Cagney gasped.
until she feared

The curtains opened, revealing the boy she saw in her dreams every single night. A boy life had chiseled into an incredibly gorgeous—and apparently filthy rich—man. A boy who had listened to her dreams, yet who'd left her in the hospital after the devastating crash without so much as a get-well balloon.

A boy who'd broken her heart, and yet, despite that, the one person she'd never stopped loving.

Jonas had returned.

Dear Reader,

Sometimes a teenage romance is simply puppy love, but every so often that first love truly is meant to last forever. My best friend, Terri, and her husband, Dan, have been together since high school—growing and changing and building a family together. They're the inspiration for this story about Cagney and Jonas. Like Terri and Dan, Cagney and Jonas are absolutely meant for each other. Soul mates. Unlike my friends (thank goodness, huh, Terri?), Cagney and Jonas have to suffer heartache, distance and estrangement before they reach their much-deserved happily ever after.

I hope you enjoy their journey back to one another, and I hope you find your happily ever after, whether in high school or later in life. I'd love to hear your soul-mate story. Please write me through my publisher, or via my Web site, www.LyndaSandoval.com.

Hugs,

Lynda Sandoval

YOU, AND
NO OTHER

LYNDA SANDOVAL

SPECIAL EDITION

Published by Silhouette Books

America's Publisher of Contemporary Romance

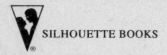

SILHOUETTE BOOKS

ISBN-13: 978-0-373-28125-1
ISBN-10:   0-373-28125-0

YOU, AND NO OTHER

Visit Silhouette Books at www.eHarlequin.com

Printed in U.S.A.

Books by Lynda Sandoval

Silhouette Special Edition

And Then There Were Three #1611
One Perfect Man #1620
The Other Sister #1851
Déjà You #1866
You, and No Other #1877

LYNDA SANDOVAL

is a former police officer who exchanged the excitement of that career for blissfully isolated days, creating stories she hopes readers will love. Though she's also worked as a youth mental health and runaway crisis counselor, a television extra, a trade-show art salesperson, a European tour guide and a bookkeeper for an exotic bird and reptile company—among other weird jobs—Lynda's favorite career, by far, is writing books. In addition to romance, Lynda writes women's fiction and young adult novels, and in her spare time, she loves to travel, quilt, bid on eBay, hike, read and spend time with her dog. Lynda also works part-time as an emergency fire/medical dispatcher for the fire department. Readers are invited to visit Lynda on the Web at www.LyndaSandoval.com, or to send mail with a SASE for reply to P.O. Box 1018, Conifer, CO 80433-1018.

This one is for Charles Griemsman,
A kick-butt editor (in a good way)
and my new friend.
I live for your hearts and smiley faces!

Prologue

Twelve years ago...

Cagney Bishop tensed when she heard the crunch of tires on the gravel drive in front of their house. She'd become so attuned to her police chief father's explosive and unpredictable behavior over the years, she could gauge the mood of the coming evening simply from how he opened and closed the doors.

Engine killed.

Door opened.

SLAM!

She winced, then quickly hid her sketch pad beneath her comforter, replacing it with a textbook and spiral notebook. She poised her pencil over the page and cocked her head to listen.

Heavy stomps.

Key in the lock.

Door creak.

SLAM!

Her shoulders sagged. So much for tonight, but oh, well. Same crap, different day, right? She shouldn't feel the least twinge of disappointment. After seventeen-plus years, did she think he'd suddenly morph into a father worthy of a Hallmark card? Dream on.

She snuggled farther into her upholstered headboard, as if she could somehow make herself a smaller target. No doubt he'd have words with Mom first, but eventually—like always—he'd wind up in her face for some trumped-up reason.

Hang in there, she told herself, vying to shake off the never-ending pall of her home life and refocus on her goals for the weeks, months, years ahead. Prom, then graduation, then she'd finally—thank God—*finally* be off to college and out from under the chief's oppressive regime. If she could just suck it up a few more weeks, which was nothing in the scheme of things. Even if it felt like an eternity…

Her door swung open much sooner than expected and hit the opposite wall, but she didn't react—a coping mechanism she'd honed to perfection over the years.

Never let him see you sweat.

After his last bout of fury, when he'd, yet again, thrown her door open so violently that the doorknob had punched into the drywall, she'd given up on the futile and repeated patch jobs. Instead, she stuffed the hole with a small, poofy pillow to soften future blows and prevent those loud, intimidating slams he seemed so fond of. Still, she wanted to yell *have a little respect for my privacy*—or better, *go the hell away*—but she never would.

Despite the lack of clatter with today's entrance, one glance into her father's reddened face told her she was in for it. It didn't help that he still wore his intimidatingly authoritative uniform, gun and all—not that he'd ever *physically* abuse any of them, but still. Sometimes she wondered if a punch would hurt less than his relentless, cutting words.

Schooling her features into nothingness,

she held his gaze. Waiting. Always best to take the defensive when dealing with an unpredictable force.

When he didn't speak, a dull thud started in her chest. He couldn't have found out about her subversive prom plans, could he? She almost scoffed aloud, even as fear clawed up her spine. Who was she kidding? He could find out anything. He had an entire police force of spies and wasn't afraid to use them, ethics be damned.

"What in the *hell* do you think you're doing?" he said finally, through clenched teeth.

Play dumb. Her gaze strayed to the books in her lap, then back to his face. "Homework, Chief?" Pretty pathetic that she couldn't bear to call her father by anything but that. Any affection she'd felt for the man had died long ago. Dad? Daddy? Those words meant nothing to her. Some kids got lucky. Other kids got *out*.

"Don't get smart with me." He yanked the little pillow out of the ruined drywall and whipped it across the room. "You know what I'm talking about."

Uh-oh. She managed a tight swallow. She probably did know. Still, the prom wasn't until tomorrow night, and it could be any number of perceived transgressions. No sense showing her hand prematurely. "If you'll just tell me—"

"Prom, Cagney." Chief started pacing—no, stalking—around the room, clenching and unclenching his fists. "Your lies, Cagney. That little Eberhardt dirtbag, *Cagney,*" he spat, his tone icy and derisive. "You thought I wouldn't find out?"

Hopefully? Well, at least not until she chose to tell him. She decided to consider his question rhetorical and not address it at all. "It's just a dance." She struggled to keep her tone light, to avoid pleading. "We're school friends, that's all. If you'd give Jonas a chance—"

"Damn it! Are you stupid?" In two strides, he loomed over her. "I forbid you to go with that criminal, do you understand?"

It took a moment for his words to sink in. "But—"

"No!" He cut off her protests with one slash of his hand through the air. "After all I've given you, all I've done for you, now this? I'd expect this kind of sneaky behavior from that worthless sister of yours, Terri. But I thought you were following in Deirdre's footsteps."

Deirdre, the "good daughter." She'd gone off and joined the FBI, making Chief proud. Cagney pushed back her initial shock that he'd even mentioned the "bad daughter," Terri, who had defied him to run off to New York City two years earlier. Since then, no one was allowed to utter her name in his presence. Apparently the unfair rule only applied to the rest of them. "I'm not following in anyone's footsteps, Chief. I have my own path. I'm just me."

He barked out an evil laugh. "Well, let me tell you how things are going to be, '*just me*,'" he said with a sneer, "because I'm going to give you a chance to redeem yourself. You have a choice."

A choice? Wow, a first. She gulped. "Okay."

"You either go off to your prom with that Eberhardt bastard, or you don't."

She blinked. "W-what do you mean?"

"I mean, instead, you'll go with someone else. Someone I approve of."

Too easy. Had to be a trap. She bit one corner of her lip and took a moment to consider what exactly he was up to, but couldn't figure it out. "Then, if that's my choice, I'll go with Jonas."

A slash of a smile split his stern face. Not a real smile, of course. She didn't remember him ever *truly* smiling. "Great. Go off with your little hoodlum." A long, thick pause ensued. "But you'll see no money from me for your college education if you do. Not a dime."

Her stomach churned violently. "Chief—!"

"Those are the terms." He let them sink in. "Because I'm a nice guy, I'll give you one more chance to make a different choice, and that college education you dream of can be yours."

To her horror, the churning rose to her throat, and she thought she might be sick right then and there. How could she choose between those awful options? Jonas or college? Bottom line, she *needed* the Chief's financial backing to get to college, and she desperately needed college for her freedom and sanity. It was too late to apply for financial assistance. Even loans, at least for the first semester, and her dad made too much money for her to qualify for any grants. But she couldn't bear another six months at home. She *had* to start classes on time.

And yet, she needed Jonas for her sanity. Prom without Jonas? Her heart rattled.

Sure, he lived in a trailer on the far side of Troublesome Gulch with a single mom who spent too much time. in the bars—the ultimate hard-luck cliché—but so what? Should he be punished for that?

Jonas was the best person she knew. Thoughtful, observant, supportive, unassuming. He rose above his circumstances with dreams and goals and the resiliency to make them come true.

He wanted to write and had already composed raw, poignant, honest poetry she kept hidden in a box at the back of her closet. Aside from Mrs. DeLuca, the art teacher at school (and also her friend Erin's mom), Jonas was the only person in the world who believed Cagney could succeed as an artist and could use her talent to help others.

He inspired her.

He loved her.

Jonas knew more about her and her farce of a home life than even her best friends. She glossed over most of that with the girls out of sheer embarrassment, but she told Jonas *everything*. They'd been forced to sneak around for years now, thanks to Chief's discrimination against anyone he deemed unworthy. As far as *he* knew, she hadn't been hanging with Jonas since before sophomore year, while in fact, she and Jonas had been in love since then.

They'd simply become experts at hiding.

Her rebellion was alive and well, but unequivocally passive.

She and Jonas had decided the prom would be their one out-in-the-open hurrah in Troublesome Gulch, a night just for the two of them and to hell with her father. They had the whole thing planned. They'd present a united front to Chief, lay out their case with cool logic, refuse to take no for an answer, and he'd eventually relent. What else could he do? Cagney was almost eighteen. It was supposed to be a magical night. Cagney and Jonas, just like fate intended.

Oh, how she'd underestimated her father. He'd rather deny her an education than see her happy with someone who didn't meet his approval.

"Well?" Chief growled.

She worried her bottom lip between her teeth.

Jonas was a long-term, big-picture type of thinker, though. Who cared about one night, one dance, in the grand scheme of things, when they had their whole future? She could explain the situation; he knew what Chief was about. Knowing Jonas, he'd probably encourage her to jump through her father's stupid hoops. The most important thing was getting to the university where they'd both been accepted, where they could spend every day together.

Jonas would get it. She just had to talk to him.

Her tension eased. "Fine. I'll call Jonas and—"

"Absolutely not."

Her eyes widened. "What?"

"I forbade you from talking to that hoodlum years ago, and although you disobeyed my orders without any regard, the rules still apply."

Her breathing shallowed. "I can't just stand him up. That's completely rude."

Her father leaned closer until she could smell the bitter precinct coffee on his breath. "You don't get it, do you? I don't care about that kid or his feelings, if he has any. You'll go to the prom with someone else, and you won't call your friends or Eberhardt before then. If you defy these terms, no college. Simple. Don't think I'm kidding."

"Chief!" She pounded her fists on the mattress at her sides. "That's not fair."

He grabbed her wrist and squeezed. "Life isn't fair, and here's a prime chance for you to learn that."

As if she didn't already know. A flash of anger emboldened her. "What happened that turned you so unbelievably cruel?" she asked in a hard whisper.

An avalanche of emotion moved over his face in a split second before his expression went stony and his tone lowered to a dangerous growl. "Yes or no, Cagney. Now. I have better things to do than play games with you."

Her chin quivered from rage despite her best efforts to keep her emotions in the deep freeze. She stiffened her spine. It would be last-minute, but she could talk to Jonas at school tomorrow, hash everything out.

"Oh, and you won't be going to school tomorrow," Chief said, as though reading her mind. "I've called the office already."

Her heart sank, and her vision swirled.

"What? You thought I wouldn't consider every angle?"

How could she? Her father was the most calculating, manipulative person she'd ever known. But this really topped all. What was the point in it? To purposefully hurt Jonas? And her? She knew Chief was a control freak, but she hadn't realized until that moment how truly mean-spirited he was.

"So?" His eyes glittered victoriously. He knew he had her. "What will it be? Prom with a boy who will never be worthy of you, or a college education? Your choice."

Everything inside her went cold. She couldn't feel. Couldn't react appropriately. She should be weeping, screaming at him like Terri would've been. Instead, she just felt numb. Trapped. Tortured. "College, Chief. Of course college. What do you think I am, some kind of an idiot?"

He released her wrist, disgust in his expression. "Considering your choice of associates, sometimes I wonder." He swaggered over to her purse, opened it, removed her cell phone, then walked to the wall and unplugged her home extension. "These go with me. Now that I know I can't trust you. Don't even try to use the computer, either. The modem is also with me."

Icy fury bubbled in her throat.

Fight it back. Fight it back.

"There is no getting around this, so don't bother trying. I'll be staying home tomorrow to monitor you until your date picks you up for prom."

"I'm not your prisoner, you know." Though sometimes she wondered.

"No, you're my daughter, who lives in *my* house and abides by *my* rules. Who will be your date?"

No answer.

"Fine." He started toward the door. "Don't go at all. I'd prefer that anyway."

"No, wait." She blew out a steadying breath. She couldn't bear the thought of sitting in this oppressive house while her best friends in the world were at prom, especially knowing it would be her father's preference. Her heart ached for Jonas, but she was backed into a corner. She supposed she could call him from the dance and have him meet her there. That was something. "I'll go stag. With my friends."

"Forget it. Only losers and sluts go stag."

"That's not true!"

He shrugged. "Name an escort or stay home."

She blew out her frustration. "Tad Rivers, I guess?" she muttered. "He asked me, and I don't think he has another date. He'd planned on going *stag*." She glared up through her lashes. "So, is he a loser because of that or does he pass your inspection? His dad's the city attorney."

"I'll call Will Rivers right now."

"I want to go in a group. With my friends. Mick and Erin and Lexy are all going together with their dates." Maybe she could get word to Jonas that he'd have to meet her there if she had the chance to rearrange plans with them. "If I can just call Lexy—"

"I'll take care of it."

"Gee, thanks. Do you even know what to say to her?"

He held up a finger. "Cut the snotty attitude. I'm doing you a favor. You should be thanking me."

Cagney clenched her fists so hard that her fingernails drew blood in her palms, but she welcomed the sting. If she couldn't go with Jonas, she was going to smuggle in the alcohol and get stinking drunk. Her father deserved that slap in the face, at least.

"Your mother said dinner is in twenty minutes."

"I'm not hungry," she muttered.

He whipped back, frowning. "I don't give a damn if you ate three lunches and you're stuffed full. Your mother cooked a meal, which is more than that worthless drunk Ava Eberhardt did tonight, I'm sure, and you'll be at the table in twenty minutes. Do I make myself clear?"

A long pause ensued, during which she contemplated defending Jonas's mother, toyed with telling Chief exactly where to go. Then she remembered her college escape plan, his invisible financial choke collar on her. He hadn't even allowed her to work a part-time job during high school, so she had no money of her own. Zippo. Not a dime. Just another way for him to keep her under his thumb.

"Yes, sir," she said, an emotionless, powerless shell.

"I'm glad to see you can be reasonable. On occasion. I won't forget your defiance, Cagney."

She met his gaze directly but managed to leach the emotion from her words. "I feel sorry for you, Chief."

His lips thinned. "Save it." And with that, he left.

Cagney's feelings were twisted and stuffed so far inside her she couldn't even cry. Her father deadened every part of her—it seemed the only way she could survive. She couldn't even trust that her feelings were real anymore. When she hurt, did she *really* hurt? She thought she felt the cold clutch of

fear sometimes, but was it truly fear or something else? How could she know? Everything was messed up inside her. She rested
her face in her hands and breathed deeply.

Any other girl might be able to go to her
mother for an ally in an argument like this,
but *her* mom—Cagney shook her head.
Look up the word passive in the dictionary,
and you'd find a picture of Mom beside the
word. She'd never defy Chief, not even to
righteously defend her daughters.

Cagney sighed.

They would pull through this, she and
Jonas.

He would get over the disappointment.
He loved her.

He'd meet her at the dance, and they'd
proceed as planned. It wouldn't be the way
they'd hoped the night would play out, but
somehow…some way, she'd explain away
all the hassle and lies and convolutions.

And Jonas, as always, would understand.

Jonas still couldn't believe how much it
cost to rent an uncomfortable penguin suit for
one measly night. It was worth it, though. For
Cagney. A mixture of excitement and dread
swirled inside him as he pulled his mom's

decrepit Monte Carlo into the circular drive in front of her house, half expecting her father to come smashing out of the door, shotgun in hand. He turned off the engine and waited, holding his breath. Nothing happened.

He studied the front of the imposing, impeccable stone house trying not to compare it to his and mom's shabby mobile home with its loose metal siding and squeaky porch stairs. Still, this house might be big, impressive from the outside, but he knew from Cagney how little love resided within its walls. He'd take his troubled but sweet mom and their rented trailer any day of the week.

To his surprise, the Bishops' porch light flicked on. He didn't know whether to take that as welcome or warning, but one thing was sure—stalling in the driveway would get him nowhere fast.

Blowing out a breath, he retrieved the orchid wrist corsage he'd picked up for Cagney at the grocery store florist and stepped out of the car. He took a moment to button his jacket and smooth his hair before heading toward the porch.

Now or never, he supposed.

The front door opened before he ever got a chance to ring the doorbell, and Chief Bishop stepped out, scowling as usual. Jonas honestly didn't know what he'd ever done to make the man despise him so much. He cleared his throat and squared his shoulders. "Sir."

"Don't 'sir' me." The man's eyebrows dipped into a deep V. "What do you think you're doing setting foot on my property?"

For a moment, the sheer rudeness of the question threw Jonas, and he couldn't formulate a response. Cagney hadn't been at school, nor had she returned any of his many phone calls or e-mails, but surely by now Chief Bishop knew who her prom date was. His mouth went dry, and he moistened his lips with a flick of his tongue to bolster his waning courage. "I'm here to pick up Cagney for the prom."

The older man's laughter fell to the stone floor of the porch like shattering icicles, cold and sharp. He stood, legs apart, arms crossed over his wide chest. "Hate to burst your bubble, but Cagney left for the prom half an hour ago with her date, Tad Rivers. And her friends. Go on home now. Get."

Jonas blinked twice, scarcely believing

what he'd just heard. "That's impossible. Cagney's my girlfriend," he blurted without thinking. "We have a date."

"Your *girlfriend*." Chief chewed on that. "Let me give you a bit of friendly advice, son. You want a girlfriend, you need to set your sights a little lower than my daughter. She's too good for you. Always has been, always will be."

Jonas felt the cruel sting, but he hiked his chin. Chief Bishop knew nothing about who Cagney was or what she wanted. "She loves me. And I love her."

"You love her?" The bastard's eyes widened. "You best show that love by staying the hell out of her way, then. Isn't there a little gal in that trailer park of yours you can *date?*" he said, imbuing the word with oily innuendo. "Whatever you're trying to get from my daughter is probably freely available in that encampment of yours."

Despite his best efforts, fury flamed inside Jonas. He'd never misused Cagney, and he never would. Beneath the stupid expensive tux, he began to sweat. "You don't know what you're talking about. I respect Cagney more than you ever have. I know she's here. Let me see her." He went to bypass the old man to get to the door, but a big hand on his chest held him back. "Cagney!" he yelled.

The hand became a fist, wadding his freshly pressed shirt into a mass of wrinkles as Chief Bishop lifted him slightly off his feet. "Go ahead, you little scumbag. Try to enter my house uninvited," Chief growled through clenched teeth. "Arresting you for trespassing would be the perfect satisfying cap to my evening."

Jonas lost his fight, and the older man took the opportunity to shove him back.

He staggered, then caught himself on the railing. Grasping on to his remaining dignity by a thread, Jonas tried in vain to smooth his shirt. "How can you live with so much hate inside you?" He couldn't quite keep the quaver out of his voice.

The old man ignored his question. "Cagney did leave you a letter before she and Tad headed for the dance. Good kid, that Tad Rivers," Chief mused. "Good *family.*" He allowed a moment for the comment to slice into Jonas like a rusty knife before pulling an envelope from his back pocket and holding it out. "I suppose you deserve to read it since she wrote it. Against my advice, mind you. My daughter owes you no explanation."

Explanation of *what?* Jonas's mind raced, and an icy sense of dread trickled through him. Eying the man warily, Jonas stepped forward and snatched the envelope. He tore into it, hoping for some clue as to why their planned "united front" had fallen so far by the wayside. Why hadn't she returned his calls? Made some attempt to warn him that all hell had busted loose? They'd always protected each other.

He scanned the letter quickly, recognized Cagney's writing. And the page had been torn from her favorite school notebook, the one with paper lined in purple that smelled of grapes if you rubbed it.

Bracing himself, Jonas read:

Dear Jonas:

I would've told you sooner, but I just didn't know how. You're a nice guy and you've been a good friend, but Tad and I started talking a few months ago, and I fell in love with him. It just… happened. It's easier on me, too, because Chief approves. I hope you understand…

He couldn't bear to read another agonizing word in front of Chief Bishop The man's gloating was nearly palpable, and the pain in Jonas's heart was too intense. He crumpled the letter in one hand and stared off to the side. After a moment, he glared at the smug man before him. "You did this."

"Cut the paranoia, boy. I had nothing to do with it. Read the letter. Cagney made her choice." His tone smoothed into an arrogant purr. "It's for the best."

"When have you ever known what was best for Cagney or any of your daughters?" Jonas snapped, his voice hoarse with tears he could hardly hold back. "None of them can stand you, and everyone in this town knows it."

Chief Bishop's face reddened. "You have your damned letter, now get the hell off my property. And don't let me see you here ever again."

"Don't worry," Jonas tossed over his shoulder as he spun and took the steps two at a time, his world collapsing around him.

But, no more.

If ever there was a last straw, he'd just received it.

It's easier on me, too, because Chief approves.

Chief approves.

Approval.

He'd exhausted himself trying to attain that ever-elusive approval, with zero luck. Facts were facts: this town had been nothing but unwelcoming, if not downright hostile, to him and his mom from the moment they'd made the mistake of setting foot in it.

Just today, the owner of one of the bars Mom frequented kicked her out because she was two dollars short for her tab.

Two measly dollars. Literally.

The man left his mom humiliated and sobbing on the curb, as if she hadn't poured enough money into that dive over the years. Jonas might not approve of his mother's behavior, but she was kind and broken and vulnerable, and her coping skills weren't the best, to put it mildly.

Now this.

All he and Mom had was each other.

That much was crystal clear.

The Gulch? Jonas was done with the whole damn place. Done. He might be poor, but he was whip smart and motivated, unlike so many of his classmates. He'd taken enough credits that he'd technically graduated in December, but had held out to go through the spring ceremony with Cagney.

His gut cramped.

As things stood, the school could send him his diploma, or keep it, for all he cared, because he never wanted to see any of his fellow students again, and that included Cagney. The only good thing about Troublesome Gulch had been her, and unbelievably, even their relationship turned out to be a lie.

Pain unlike any he'd ever felt seared through him. He needed to escape this hellhole as soon as possible. That was the benefit of living in a minuscule month-to-month rental, though. Not much to pack. If he had anything to say about it, he and his mother would be boxed up and out of this nightmare town tonight, and he'd never look back. He'd find a place for them to live where people judged you for what was in your heart, not your bank account. He'd work and he'd study and he'd show them all just how wrong they were about him.

One day, so help him God…

Jonas chucked the orchid corsage out of his window, clear plastic container and all, then spun gravel leaving the Bishop property. Who cared if doing so meant another point against him with Chief? None of that mattered anymore.

The prepaid cell phone he'd scrimped and saved for rang, and a stupid spark of hope had him wrestling it from his jacket to check the caller ID. Maybe, just maybe—

Tad Rivers.

Betrayal lanced through him, stealing his breath.

He ignored the rings and waited until the secondary tone told him he had a new message, then dialed in to listen to it.

Cagney.

From *Tad's* phone.

Stars swirled in his head. So, it was true. All of it. She'd gone with Tad and didn't even tell him. She'd let him waste money on a tux and flowers, then humiliate himself in front of Chief. How could *she,* of all people, do that to him?

"Jonas," the message said, "please, please answer your phone. I want to talk to you about this. To explain. I'll call you back. Okay? Please answer."

Yeah, she'd call him back. Sure she would.

From *Tad Rivers's* phone.

With his temples pounding, he glanced down at the letter that had nearly ripped the heart from his chest. Tears blurred his vision, and he wiped angrily at them with the back of one hand.

Done. Finished. Finito.

The words on those pages were all the explanation he needed from Cagney Bishop, now or ever.

Hadn't his mom always told him love couldn't be trusted?

Chapter One

Present day...

Cagney glanced around the large parking area of High Country Medical Center at the snaking vehicles and foot traffic slithering slowly in. She couldn't believe how many people were showing up for a stupid press conference. Then again, this *was* Troublesome Gulch, Colorado, where curiosity reigned. Where else would a simple media event merit this level of police presence?

She adjusted her gun belt to rest more comfortably on her hip bones, waved at one of her fellow officers who'd been assigned to work the event, too, then checked her watch. Barely nine o'clock in the morning, and she was already bored out of her mind. Go figure. Just another day in the life of Officer Cagney Bishop.

She hated crowd control almost as much as she hated traffic duty. In fact, she hated most of her duties, unless they included dealing with disadvantaged kids or truly helping people, and honestly, how often did that happen?

Inside, she groaned. How many years until she could retire? She began calculations in her head, just to pass the time.

As if sensing her need for a break in the monotony of a job that fit her like a cheaply-made dress, Cagney's cell phone rang. She freed it from the pouch on her duty belt, checked the caller ID, then smiled and flipped it open. "Hey, Faith. How's the baby?"

Faith Montesantos Austin had given birth to her and Brody's first daughter three months earlier and was riding out the tail end of leave from her job as counselor at Troublesome Gulch High School. They'd named the baby Mickie, after Faith's late sister who died in the prom night crash along with Tad, Kevin and Randy.

"She's perky and great, as usual. Woke me up three times last night, though, so she's fat-bellied and chipper, while I'm beat, bloated and bitter."

"Ugh."

"Tell me." Faith groaned. "It's why they have to make babies cute, you know."

"Puppies, too."

"So true. Huh, Hope?" The scruffy puppy Brody had given her during his marriage proposal barked once in the background. Faith laughed, then asked, "What are you up to? Are you coming by?"

When duty allowed, Cagney stopped in for a morning coffee visit to keep Faith sane during her extended maternity leave.

Faith's tone turned plaintive. "I need adult contact, Cag. Girl talk, someone to reassure me that the baby weight really *is* melting away. I mean, my God, have you seen *Erin?*" she added, referring to their close mutual friend, Erin DeLuca, a Troublesome Gulch firefighter. "Granted, she had Nate Jr. a few months before Mickie's grand entrance, but she looked like an Olympic athlete freakin' three weeks after she gave birth. *So* not fair."

"True, but remember, she only gained

nineteen pounds with her pregnancy and she's a workout maniac."

"Casey Laine Bishop, are you calling me a slug?"

Cagney laughed softly. No one ever called her Casey anymore. "Not at all, hon. Erin's just in a different physical class than most of us. We have to accept it and move on, or we'll fall into the body image self-loathing pit and never scratch our way out."

"Lucky wench, that Erin. It's a good thing I love her so much, or I'd hate her."

"Don't hate her because she's bionic," Cagney teased.

"Seriously, I'm regretting every single time I uttered the word *supersize* during those nine months of blinding French-fry cravings and zero self-control." Faith sighed. "So, now that I'm totally depressed *and* fat, are you coming over, or what?"

"Can't. Sorry. Chief assigned me to crowd control at the hospital, oh, joy." She rolled her eyes.

"The hosp— Oh! I'd forgotten that hoopla was today." Mickie started fussing in the background, and Faith shushed her gently. "What's up with the new wing anyway? Any insider info?"

"None." Cagney raised her chin to ac-knowledge the hand signal from the cop working traffic control at the entrance about fifty yards away from her, then waved a sleek, black limousine past the barricade she guarded. The mystery guest of honor, of course. Who else rode around in a stretch limo in Troublesome Freakin' Gulch?

She strained for a peek through the heavily tinted windows but saw nothing. Her hat brim and dark sunglasses didn't help. "Cops don't rate insider info. Not this cop, at least. Anyway, surprise benefactor, surprise wing, blah blah blah. Supposedly something that will put Troublesome Gulch on the map."

"Ooh," Faith mocked. "I swear, they're always trying to put Troublesome Gulch on one stupid map or the other, and yet our claim to fame remains being 'that mountain town with the horrible prom night tragedy from way back when.' Sorry for the ugly reminder," she said quickly, "but really, all this munici-pal social climbing is futile and annoying."

"Believe me, I agree. But you know how old Walt loves his publicity," Cagney added wryly, referring to the camera-loving city manager. "I'll fill you in as soon as I get any kind of scoop whatsoever. It'll probably be anticlimactic after all the buildup, though."

"I don't know why they've been so secretive," Faith said, her tone peevish. "Don't they grasp the fact that this is a small town? We're supposed to know everyone else's business. It's part of the benefits package."

Cagney snickered. "I guess the moneyman—or woman—wanted it this way."

"Yeah, but why?"

"Who knows? Rich people can be freaky and demanding. And when you're donating an entire wing to a hospital, you get whatever you ask for. We're talking millions."

"I wonder how much, exactly?"

"No clue. More than I'll ever see in this lifetime, that's for sure." She paused to watch the tail end of the limo disappear into the underground garage that had been secured for its private use, as if the First Lady herself had donated the wing. "You have to admit, all talk of maps aside, this *is* the most exciting thing that's happened in Troublesome Gulch in a while."

"But that's not saying much." Faith sighed again. "Well, call me as soon as you know something juicy. All I have on my agenda is laundry, laundry and more laundry. Who knew a baby would go through so many clothes?"

"You have my sympathy. Just wait until she's a teenager."

"Hush your mouth. She'll always be my precious baby."

A pang of envy struck Cagney's middle. "You know I'd switch places with you in a minute."

"I'll call you at 3:00 a.m. and remind you of those words," Faith said, her tone wry.

"Okay, never mind." Cagney chuckled. An electric excitement rippled through the press area, and at the same time her radio crackled with conversation. She tilted her ear to her shoulder mic to listen; the dog and pony show was about to get started. "Gotta go. Kiss that little sweetie for me."

She hung up without waiting for an answer, then slipped the phone back into its holder. After securing her barricades, she moved closer so she didn't miss anything. Faith would kill her if she didn't memorize every single detail for later.

From the curtained-off area behind the outdoor dais, Jonas Eberhardt listened dispassionately as the city manager used every effusive suck-up phrase known to man during his blustery, prolonged introduction. Jonas shook his head with disgust. The man sure liked to hear himself talk.

Tuning out the blowhard, Jonas tried to focus on this moment he'd been anticipating for more than a decade. He'd fantasized about it, dreamed it, visualized it, and yet so far, it fell short of what he'd expected. He'd begun orchestrating this revenge plot almost since he'd driven away, brokenhearted, from Cagney Bishop's house all those years ago, and he'd always planned to revel in every single second. He had pictured spending this day lording over the Gulchers in repayment for having always passed unfair judgment on him and his mother.

It wasn't working that way.

To his shock, everyone so far had been gracious.

Genuinely, or so it seemed. Certainly it had something to do with the fact that he had money now, his inner cynic whispered. He should be happy they were welcoming, regardless of the reason, but he couldn't seem to muster up the emotion. Wealthy or not, he still didn't belong.

With a yank on one diamond-and-platinum-cuff-linked sleeve, then the other, he frowned at his inner turmoil. Throughout all of his extensive planning, he hadn't foreseen the strangeness of being back in the town he despised after so many years. It defied simple description. After all he'd accomplished in the computer world, he hadn't banked on feeling like that same unwanted outsider, that shame-filled kid who'd tried so hard to blend in.

Shoot, with the staggering amount of money he'd just handed over to the hospital board, they ought to give him the key to the damn city and rename the main road after him. And yet, a small part of him felt somehow…undeserving.

Which was bull, of course. But the town stripped him of confidence, seemingly without trying.

The hand-tailored suit he wore cost more than twelve months' rent on that dilapidated trailer he'd spent his high-school years living in. So why did he still feel like the lonely, misjudged teenager from the bad side of town wearing secondhand jeans from the thrift shop?

He flinched. *Stop it.*

The surreal feelings churning inside him

threatened to ruin everything. He clenched his jaw and fought to shake them off. The fact was, he'd more than succeeded in his life despite overwhelming odds, and no insular little Podunk town should be able to diminish that, not even Troublesome Gulch.

Cagney's town.

Cagney.

A familiar flash of pain, followed by a roar of self-preserving anger. He let his eyes drift shut for a moment. Okay, she was the problem, and the honest part of him knew it.

He had loved her more than anything in this world, opened up to her like he hadn't done with anyone before or since, and she'd ruthlessly trampled his heart. He never wanted to feel that kind of pain again.

The merciless part of him hoped she still lived here, though he knew she'd hear about this spectacle either way. And when it was all over, he hoped she felt this precision cut all the way down to the bone. God knew, his wounds at her hand were still festering, and paybacks were...well, everyone knew exactly what they were.

He *had* learned that her bastard of a father still ran his dictatorship in the Gulch, and knowing this whole thing would infuriate the old man provided some consolation. But mostly, he focused on Cagney.

And yet, a twinge of…something…nagged at him.

Regret? Conscience? Self-doubt? Whatever it was, the fact that it detracted from this all-important day annoyed him. He deserved this. More importantly, *she* deserved this.

Being back in the Gulch brought forth the kid he used to be, and the problem was, it shook him. He never thought he'd end up being the kind of man who'd seek retribution, but prom night—that deep betrayal— had killed something innocent inside him. His heart had shattered and his soul hardened in one fell swoop, and he'd vowed to show them all one day that Jonas Eberhardt couldn't be shoved aside like so much trash.

Every single decision he'd made in his adult life had led him toward this day, this place, this chance to subtly smack down a few people and set the record straight. He'd *lived* for this goal, worthy or not, so he'd better quash the unexpected doubt immediately or he'd miss out on the glory moment.

Reaching into his jacket pocket, he wrapped his hand around the talisman he always carried. In previous times of self-doubt, it had always given him strength of purpose. Power. Now it fueled him for what lay ahead. An eye for an eye, just as it should be. He'd make his point—one only Cagney would fully grasp—and then he'd hightail it out of Troublesome Gulch for the second time and never look back.

Score: even.

This town had made it abundantly clear what they thought of him twelve years ago, and his current financial status wouldn't change that—at least not for him. Today, despite his unexpected maelstrom of feelings and no matter how many millions it cost him, the last word would be his. The awkward feelings would dissipate eventually, and money had never mattered to him anyway.

Cagney mostly tuned out Walt Hennessy— master of verbosity—as he dragged out the introduction until it made the worst of Oscar- night speeches seem like breezy, witty blips.

Get on with it, she wanted to yell.

The table in front of the podium held some large lumpy thing covered with billowy, red fabric, and she could see most eyes focused on that rather than Hennessy. No doubt it was an architect's rendering of the proposed supersecret wing. Surely *that* would be more interesting than old Walt's incessant prattle.

After several more minutes of pointless effusing, Hennessy nodded to his four underlings, who were poised to unveil the model. They moved into position, each grasping a corner of the red cloth.

"Without further ado, I'd like to bring out the man who is making this all possible, one of Troublesome Gulch's own."

Wait a minute—a Gulcher? That was an unexpected twist. Cagney's curiosity was piqued, and she angled a bit closer. Who could it be? More importantly, how had this mysterious Gulcher walked amongst them and still kept the secret? Everybody knew secrets were impossible in the Gulch.

"Before that, however, I'd like you all to take a look at what will be the crowning jewel of High Country Medical Center." He paused dramatically, then spoke in a booming voice, arms spread wide. "The Ava Eberhardt Memorial Art Therapy Wing. Gentlemen?"

The cloth billowed back, and everyone erupted into applause and cheers and excited conversation. Cameras flashed. People

shouldered closer, craning their necks and
jockeying for a better view.

All Cagney could do was stand frozen and
replay Hennessy's incomprehensible words
in her brain.

Ava Eberhardt?

Memorial?

Art therapy?

The thud of her heart literally hurt; she
couldn't feel her extremities. Her mind raced
and her blood chilled. Jonas's mother hadn't
exactly been an icon of Troublesome Gulch
society—far from it. So, who could the benefactor be but—

"And, the man making it all possible,
Troublesome Gulch's own prodigal son, Mr.
Jonas Eberhardt."

Cagney gasped. Stars filled her vision until
she feared she'd pass out.

The curtains behind the elaborate outdoor
dais opened revealing none other than the
boy she saw in her dreams every single night.
A boy life had chiseled into an incredibly
gorgeous—and apparently filthy rich—man.
A boy who had listened to and encouraged
all her dreams of creating art and helping
people, of combining the two into a career,
yet who'd left her in the hospital after the

devastating prom night crash without so much as a phone call or a get-well balloon. A boy who'd broken her heart, and yet, despite that, the one person she'd never stopped loving.

Jonas had returned.

Her knees melted to nothing. She wobbled toward the nearest parked vehicle—a Ford pickup—and sank onto the front bumper, sucking air and trying to regain her equilibrium. A myriad of emotions swirled through her. Excitement. Fear. Wonder. Resentment. Anger.

Why?

Why had Jonas come back after all these years? Why—and how—was he funding, of all things, an art therapy wing at the hospital when that career field had been *her* dream, not his? More importantly, why hadn't he cared enough to tell her?

The big part of her that would always love Jonas wanted to believe this grand gesture was somehow for her, which warmed her soul. But it also made no sense. Another more resentful, less logical part felt as though he'd intentionally stolen her dream. Or worse, as if he were rubbing the failures of her life in her face. Bringing into sharp relief the fact that she hadn't been able to cut it, had abandoned her art and settled for a job she never wanted in the first place.

But why would he do that? How would he even know?

She hadn't seen nor heard from him in twelve long, empty years.

Every one of her stuffed-down regrets boiled to the surface. She wanted to run. Hide. Scream. She wanted to tear off this stupid uniform and demand a life do-over.

With considerable effort, Cagney pulled herself together.

She needed to talk to Jonas privately before her wild imagination created yet more scenarios that didn't exist, before she did something rash that she'd regret. Because, more than anything else, she wanted a second chance at the conversation that should have happened more than a decade earlier.

Chapter Two

Jonas addressed the assemblage much more quickly than Hennessy had introduced him, or at least it felt that way. He fake smiled his way through a ceremonial groundbreaking, mostly for the media, then made himself and the architect who'd designed the new wing available for one-on-one questions during a meet-and-greet reception.

That part only took about an hour, but by the end, he was emotionally drained and ready to retreat to his hotel room in nearby Crested Butte. The whole day hád been… weird. A letdown. Not at all what he'd expected. The glow of smug satisfaction he'd anticipated over the years simply hadn't materialized.

Confused and lost, he said his requisite goodbyes as swiftly as possible, then made his way down the ramp to where the limo waited in the underground garage. His handmade Italian leather shoes echoed on the pavement in the cavernous and largely empty concrete structure. He loosened his tie as he walked, then said to hell with it and whipped the thing off altogether.

After inhaling deeply, he blew out a long breath, ran his hands through his hair—and that's when he saw her.

Cagney. Standing next to his limo.

He stopped dead as—much to his surprise—a wave of uncertainty assailed him.

His Cagney, all grown-up and more beautiful than ever, stood right within reach. Her hair was pulled back, but wisps of it danced around her face. She fiddled her fingers together, finally settling on crossing her arms—just like she'd always done when she was nervous around him. Was she nervous? When he didn't move, she offered him a brave, small smile. Happy? Anxious?

Everything inside him twisted and tightened. He wasn't supposed to feel like this. He was supposed to hate her.

Her lips looked the same. Did they taste the same? And her thick, blond hair...would it still feel like mink against his palms?

"Hi," she said, her tone choked off.

His well-honed composure crumbled, and all he wanted in that split second was *her.* Some uncontrollable insanity urged him to toss his vengeful plans out the window, then wrap her in his arms and whisper that everything was okay. They were adults now, and Chief Bishop no longer had a say in their choices. That evil SOB didn't even have to be a part of their lives if they didn't want him to be.

Drunk on impulse and long-dead romantic dreams, he took two steps forward before he noticed her outfit: a Troublesome Gulch Police uniform. It stunned him like an uppercut from out of nowhere. So much for excising Chief from their lives.

Oh, yeah. They didn't *have* a life together. Remember? Never had, never would.

Ugly reality settled over him like armor, which was exactly what he needed to survive this unexpected encounter. He cleared his throat, hardened his heart. "What are you doing here?"

"I live here," she said, easily.

He didn't want to hear the unspoken, *and you don't,* but the implication ribboned through his brain unbidden. He raised one eyebrow and huffed. "Well, you have my sympathies in that respect."

Her smile faded into a look of confusion, which quickly transformed into something far more invasive and insightful. She cocked her head to the side, studying him with those laser-blue eyes that had always been able to see into his soul.

Good thing he'd developed a nearly impenetrable emotional shell over the years. Still, his breathing shallowed. "What?"

"Nice speech out there."

He didn't need her approval. "What do you want, Cagney?"

"At this point? A simple answer to a simple question."

He exhaled with impatience. "Make it fast. I have meetings," he lied.

"Oh, I will." She paused until he looked at her. "If you hate Troublesome Gulch so much, then why did you bring your zillions here, to our hospital? And an art therapy wing, of all things." Her tone was soft, unassuming. Her words were not. "It's pretty puzzling."

She knew him.

She'd always known him.

He didn't have to put up with this. After a moment's hesitation, he shouldered gently past her and opened the limo's back door.

"Don't you have a driver to do that kind of thing for you?"

He threw his tie inside the plush vehicle, then shrugged out of his jacket and did the same with it. He turned to face her, disconcerted by how close she stood. He could smell the unique perfume of her skin, etched into his memory. Pine and wildflowers and woman. "I don't believe in making people wait on me just because I earn more money than they do. I'm perfectly capable of opening my own door."

"Fair enough." She shrugged. "But then, why the limo? Isn't that sort of service the whole point?"

Valid question. Damn it. He silently castigated himself, then muttered, "Seemed fitting under the circumstances."

"Ah, the circumstances." Another pointed pause. "You haven't answered my first question. Why here? Why this particular donation?"

Revenge was the honest answer. An eye for an eye. Paybacks. He wanted to hurt her like she'd hurt him. Worse. Of course, he couldn't come right out and say that.

He dragged his gaze over the length of her body, ending at her face. "Maybe I thought you'd followed your dreams, though by the look of your work attire, I'm obviously mistaken."

Her cheeks reddened as though he'd slapped her.

A surge of remorse bolted through him.

Then again, why should it? After the way she'd destroyed him, he shouldn't feel bad about anything he said to her.

"You could've asked." She shrugged. "I've always been here. Number's in the book."

Right. He struggled for a plausible explanation. "Maybe I did it for you, Cagney. Ever thought of that?" He held both palms up. "My error, since you seem to have taken a different path."

Seemingly impervious to his icy demeanor, she hiked her chin. "Use your words as weapons all you want, but I don't believe that."

He frowned, feeling off-kilter and not liking it one bit. She was so together, so steady. "Don't believe what?"

She gestured toward the hospital. "That you'd do something like…this art therapy wing…for me."

His gaze narrowed. "Yeah? Why not? Finally learn to hate me from your old man?"

She paused again, but he could see the slight tremor of her hands. "If anyone has learned hate and anger, it's obviously you."

It pained him that he couldn't deny it. He looked away.

"I don't believe you'd do something this…huge…for me because you never even talked to me again, never let me explain what happened," she said in a level tone.

"Which is what you wanted."

"No, it wasn't." She spread her arms, the first show of frustration pinking her cheeks. "You actually switched colleges, Jonas. After everything you and I had gone through to get there together. You declined your hard-earned financial aid package and disappeared. Never told a soul where you'd gone. Forgive me for stating the obvious, but clearly it was what *you* wanted."

A boost of anger emboldened him. Now he was to blame? Frowning, he leaned closer and lowered his tone. "Why would I stay in touch after what happened? Go through with our so-called plans? Your feelings were abundantly clear."

To her credit, she held her ground. "They *weren't*. You never gave me the chance to discuss my feelings before you hightailed it out of here, forwarding address unknown." She shook her head. "The going got a little tough, Jonas, and you ran. Without a single word."

"That's bull."

"Why can't you own up to it?"

Now he was pissed. "I have to go."

"Going getting tough again?"

"Drop it. I'm not kidding."

She reached out and grabbed his forearm, not cowed by his obvious anger. "I'm not done."

"Then finish," he snapped, pulling away from her grasp.

Those blue eyes of hers went round. "You never visited me in the hospital after the crash on prom night. Not once. Why?"

Jonas held her gaze, but not easily, and he didn't say a word. Truth was, he hadn't known. Not right away. He remembered every minute detail of the morning he'd read about the crash, more than two years after it happened. Some kind of exposé in the Sunday paper about teen driving dangers.

He remembered gripping the newsprint so tightly that it had torn, and not being able to take a breath until he knew Cagney had survived. And then breaking down…and hating himself for it.

"Fine, don't answer." Her eyes shone, but she didn't waver. "Doesn't matter anyway, because I know the truth. I lived it. You just flat out vanished when I needed you more than ever. Our love was obviously a lie—"

"No kidding."

That startled her, but she covered it quickly. "So, you see? It's only logical. With all that evidence, why would I believe that you'd cater to a decade-old dream of mine now?"

Decade-old, huh? He supposed he should be happy about her dreams going to dust, but strangely, he wasn't. She was born to be an artist, and artists created. Her abandoning that God-given gift felt like a death, and he'd stomached more than his share of that recently. But she didn't deserve his compassion. He needed to remember that. "I got all the explanation I needed that night."

"Explanation from whom? Chief?"

He hesitated, questioning his motivation for the first time ever. "From your actions," he said, although, admittedly, Chief's words had a lot to do with it.

"And that was enough for you? Chief? Assumptions? My so-called actions?" she asked, with a small, humorless laugh. "Without ever talking to me again? You said you would love me forever, Jonas."

"I—" His gut twisted as the ugly night rushed back at him. In his blinding, teenage, lovesick anger, he'd truly never looked at the whole thing from all perspectives. He *had* loved her, more than life itself. But it hardly mattered now, and he wouldn't stand here and let her manipulate him into looking like the bad guy. "Talking would've been a waste of time—" he took in her uniform and couldn't hold back the derision "—obviously. Just let it go. It's over, Cagney. It's *been* over."

"Okay, it's over. But don't you think we should talk? Get some closure at least?"

"Closure's overrated." Shaking his head in disgust, he got into the limo and tried to shut the door.

She held it open, but her blue eyes had lost some of their hopefulness. "Run away if you have to. But you're wrong, Jonas. About me, about that night. About so many things, and it just makes me…"

"What?" he asked in a belligerent tone, daring her to say *she* was angry.

She seemed to consider her words, but finally, she shrugged. "It makes me sad."

Unexpected. But he had to hold on to his purpose. Now he was in the wrong and she was sad? What about his pain? His own heartbreak? His body flashed over with that familiar, blinding bitterness that had ruled his world for so many years. "Wow, I'm sorry you feel *sad,* Cagney," he snapped. "By the way, how was prom with Tad?"

She flinched visibly, looking at him as if she hadn't a clue who he was anymore. "My God. Tad is *dead,* Jonas. And so are three of my best friends in the world. I can't believe you'd throw that in my face."

He clenched his fists, silently chastising himself. He'd known that, of course. His comment had been knee-jerk, heartless and unwarranted. Damn it. He should apologize—right then and there. He knew it, and yet his throat constricted until he couldn't say the words.

"Look, I thought we could talk this out, but it's obvious you're not willing to listen to any of my explanations about the past. I will say this about the future, though," Cagney said, softly. "If you donated that hospital wing in some inexplicable attempt to hurt me, you wasted your money." A wistful half smile lifted the corners of her lips. "And, then again, you didn't. There are a lot of needy kids in pain—a lot of people who will benefit from what you're doing here. Sorry if that's not what you intended."

He scowled, completely off his game. How in the hell had his revenge plan backfired so monumentally? "You have no idea about my intentions. You might recall, I was one of those needy kids in pain, thanks to this town. To your father, in particular." *And you*, he wanted to say. He settled for a snide tone as he added, "But I guess I shouldn't speak ill of the old bastard now that you play on his team."

A shadow of shame crossed her expression. Just as quickly, it vanished, replaced by a look of penetrating recognition. "Okay, point taken. I'm a cop and you don't approve. Take a number, get in line." She paused. "So, how's the writing going, Jonas?"

The jab hit home. He struggled for footing on his own slippery rock of pain, his own shame, his own purpose—if he had one anymore. Truth was, he hadn't written a word in twelve years. Easier to point out her failings than face his own. "Tell me, Cagney, how long did it take him to browbeat you into submission? Into giving up everything you ever wanted for the almighty badge and gun?"

Her gaze went distant. "Stop it."

He ignored her. "Unless everything we talked and dreamed about was just another elaborate set of Cagney Bishop lies, and you never wanted to be an artist in the first place. Maybe our whole so-called relationship was bull, beginning to end, and you were more your father's daughter than I realized. What was I, then, other than the town fool?" he asked in a rough tone. "Your little wrong-side-of-the-tracks experiment? Every rich Gulch girl wants to get with a bad boy, right?"

Cagney yanked her hand from the doorjamb as though the metal had shocked her. Her eyes went round, filled with tears. "Oh, my God. I get it now. I can't believe this."

"Believe what," he snapped, hating to see her cry.

"You…hate me," she whispered, her voice quavering. "I never would've imagined it, but *you* actually hate *me*."

The anguish in her tone tore him up. This couldn't be happening. It wasn't supposed to go this way. The past twelve years zipped through his vision, like the view out of a bus window as he fought to slam on the brakes. He grappled for something familiar to get him through. Anger. Anger always worked, didn't it?

"Jonas, say it," she persisted, her voice wavering. "Be a man and say it if it's true. You hate me. Right?"

Hate implied passion, and passion was way too close to love. Not going there. What he felt for Cagney wasn't what he expected upon his return, but he didn't dare examine it too closely. Not in front of her, at least. So, he did the only thing he knew to do anymore: he retreated. "Nope." He grabbed the door handle and formulated the lie that felt like poison at the back of his throat. "It's worse than that, Officer Bishop. I just don't care."

He slammed the door, desperate to escape, then pressed the speaker button and told his driver, Leon, to hit it.

"You've become just like him," came Cagney's muffled voice through the closed window, "and you can't even see it. God, Jonas, how could you have let him win?"

His entire body began to shake, as everything he'd based his adult life on disintegrated before his eyes. He had to get away from the disaster this day—his whole world—had become. Had to get away from Cagney and her excruciatingly clear insights.

Could he have misread the situation all along?

No. Not going there, either.

The engine sprang to life, and Cagney stumbled backward from the limo, wrapping her arms around her middle. He knew she couldn't see him through the dark window, but she never took those piercing eyes off it anyway. He watched as one tear spilled over and coursed down her soft cheek, and yet she stood in stoic silence, not bothering to wipe it away.

I am not like that bastard, he thought, his jaw tight, head pounding. But it felt like a lie, and that killed him. He pressed his palm to the glass and let the regret for everything they'd lost, everything it was far too late to get back, wash over him. The whole fiasco might be funny if it weren't so damn tragic.

Twelve years ago, he'd walked blindly into a well-set trap of blame and anger and resentment, and he'd been stuck there ever since. Now he had nothing good left inside him, nor did he have Cagney. And there was no going back.

Wouldn't Chief Bishop be thrilled?

"I don't hate you," Jonas whispered, as the only woman he'd ever loved grew smaller and smaller in the distance. "But it's way too late to fix that now."

Chapter Three

It had taken an emergency pity party with Lexy, Erin and Faith, two extralarge pizzas, a box of Godiva chocolates and three bottles of wine, but she'd done it. Merely two days after her confrontation with Jonas, Cagney had regained her footing enough to set some ideas of her own in motion.

If Jonas thought she would simply hide and lick her wounds after their clash at the press conference, he was sadly mistaken. Life had hardened him, no doubt about that, but she'd toughened up, too. Enough to know that a large part of his armor was for self-protection. She knew him well enough to see past the cold veneer to the vulnerable guy inside, no matter how much he wanted to pretend that person no longer existed.

She'd poked around and learned that he'd earned his fortune doing something with computers and would be in Troublesome Gulch until the hospital wing was finished, which meant months. Perfect. They might never be a couple again, but by the time he left, they would be friends if it killed her. They'd have their closure, if nothing else. How exactly to break through his steel shell and make all that happen… well, she wasn't sure yet. But she'd figure out a way.

This wasn't over between them.

Not by a long shot.

She'd just finished her patrol shift and had stopped by the city building to drop off some paperwork at the human resources department. As she walked by the conference room, she caught the sound of her father's angry voice. It surprised her enough to stop her in her tracks. Cold and in command was more his style—at least in public. Had to keep up that image, after all.

Pausing out of sight by the door, she

leaned her head back against the brick wall and eavesdropped.

"Look, the hospital wing is one thing—"

"It's a *great* thing," Walt Hennessy said.

"Whatever. The point is, we don't have the available space, nor do we have the need, for some idiotic youth center on top of that," her father said. "If there are displaced teens loitering about this town, we need to ticket them instead of rewarding their poor behavior with a fun place to hang out."

"Sorry to disagree, Chief Bishop," came none other than Jonas's voice, not sounding sorry at all, "but statistically, towns with designated after-school hangouts—especially for the underprivileged kids whose families might not be able to afford involving them in school or community sponsored activities like sports—have far lower crime rates."

Chief and Jonas in a room together?

Yeah, Cagney wasn't going anywhere.

"Well, thank you for the lesson on crime, Eberhardt," Chief said, barely able to hold back his sneer. Clearly, he didn't appreciate being one-upped by the kid he'd effectively run out of town. "I guess you'd know."

"That I would. Hence my vested interest."

Chief's disgust threaded through his words. "Right. However, I might point out that I have a helluva lot more experience with law enforcement than you do."

"This isn't about law enforcement, Chief," Mayor Ron Blackman interjected. "It's about serving the needs of our community, and Jonas has an excellent point."

Cagney grinned, in spite of herself. The fact that the city leaders were on a first-name basis with Jonas—and on his side—had to be killing Chief. Priceless.

Blackman continued, "We need to give these kids something to do besides causing trouble."

"Isn't that what their parents are for?" Chief barked.

"Bill," Walt Hennessy said, his tone chastising. "As one of the most prominent members of our community, your attitude is surprising. I don't understand why you're so against such a positive improvement for the Gulch. You more than anyone should know that not every child has the advantage of involved parents like yourself."

Like Chief? Cagney thought, muffling a snort. Boy, Hennessy had no clue how off base he was. She honestly couldn't believe

Chief had managed to hide his true nature from an entire city for so many years.

"Well, then, the neglectful parents need to be punished somehow," Chief sputtered. "Why should we have to cater to these people?"

"Because *these people* are citizens of Troublesome Gulch," the mayor said, his tone indignant. "And Troublesome Gulch isn't a prison, nor is it some elitist country-club community. It's a town in which people of all socioeconomic levels are welcome. No one appointed us judge, jury and executioner. We aren't the moral police, either."

"It's our job to provide services to the citizens," one of the female city council members said, which—Cagney knew— would enrage her father even more. He hated to be contradicted by women. "*All* the citizens. Perhaps you've lost a bit of perspective, Chief Bishop. A lot of those parents you refer to as neglectful simply have to work more than one job to make ends meet."

Glee bubbled up in Cagney's throat. She smacked a palm over her mouth and swallowed to avoid busting into laughter and getting caught spying. But, man, she loved witnessing her father outnumbered and outwitted.

"Well, the fact remains, we don't have available space in the areas zoned for such business," Chief said, his tone stiff. "It's a moot point. Is there even money left in this year's budget for nonsense like this, Walt?"

"I'll be funding the majority of it," Jonas said, shooting down that argument.

A flash of inspiration struck Cagney, and she jolted.

Wait one minute.

This was her chance, staring her in the face.

She could subtly stand up to her father, in front of witnesses, *and* set her plan with Jonas into motion by offering one simple suggestion. She'd pay dearly for this later with Chief, but who the hell cared? What could he do—fire her? She wasn't his minor child anymore. She turned into the doorway and rapped her knuckles on the open door.

Jonas, Chief, Walt Hennessy, Mayor Blackman and the entire city council glanced toward her at the sound. She smiled. "Sorry to interrupt. I was walking by and happened to catch some of your debate. I didn't mean to eavesdrop," she fibbed, "but I think I might have an excellent solution."

"Officer Bishop, don't you have duties to

attend to?" her father asked in a voice as cold and stinging as dry ice.

"As a matter of fact, no," she said, saccharine sweet. "I'm just off shift."

The mayor's chair scraped back, and he stood. "Come in, come in." He glanced toward the council. "I'm sure you all know Chief Bishop's youngest daughter, Cagney, one of our esteemed police officers."

Nods and murmured hellos followed.

Cagney didn't know if she would use the word *esteemed* to describe her half-hearted contribution to public safety, but whatever. It meant a paycheck every two weeks.

"Have a seat," Blackman said. "What brainstorm have you come up with, dear? Goodness knows, we're just going in circles here and could use a fresh perspective."

As she took a seat, she glanced surreptitiously at both her father and Jonas. Chief looked red-faced and ready to blow a gasket, and Jonas? Confused and more than a little intrigued. Maybe a tad annoyed, too, but so be it. She'd had enough of impossible men to last her ten lifetimes.

Steepling her hands on the table before her, she addressed the eager members of the group, letting her gaze pass over the two men who probably wished she'd never happened to come by. "As you all know, I purchased and renovated the old horse saddle plant several years ago."

"And you did a fine job," Hennessy blustered.

As if he knew. She smiled anyway. "Thank you. What you all might not know is this— I received approval from the building inspectors to use the space as residential property once I'd finished, but it's still in an area of town zoned for business. And the building is extremely large, of course, having been a manufacturing plant."

"Three stories tall, isn't it, Cagney?" the mayor asked.

She nodded. "More than fifteen thousand square feet, all told. I chose to live on the second and third floors, and I left the street level floor unfinished. It's just over five thousand square feet of wide open warehouse space."

"What's your point, Cagney?" her father growled. "We're having a meeting here, if you hadn't noticed."

Walt frowned at him. "For God's sake, Bill, let the woman talk. She's not a child anymore."

"She *is* my employee."

"Yes, well, right now she's off duty and she's here as a citizen of Troublesome Gulch," Mayor Blackman snapped. "So let her speak her piece."

She didn't even look at her father. "My *point* is, I would be more than happy to allow the city use of the street-level space to build the youth center you're discussing, since, as Chief says, we're a bit short on free space in the city proper. Like Jonas, I've thought for years now that we need a teen center in the Gulch."

Excitement rippled through the room.

"That's ridiculous," Chief said. "You don't want the town's riff-raff loitering in the same building as your home. The place will need an almost constant police presence."

He was falling right into her trap. It was almost too easy. "Makes it convenient, then, since I happen to be a police officer. And I relate well with disadvantaged teens, none of whom I consider riffraff. As a matter of fact—" she glanced at the council members "—I'd be willing to hand over my patrol duties and take a full-time assignment at the youth center, since Chief thinks we need round-the-clock law enforcement there. I've worked as a resource officer at the high school. I know a lot of these kids."

"Oh, Cagney, are you sure?" Blackman asked. "You're such a valuable member of the force."

She choked back a scoff: "I'm more than sure. Most of the cities and towns in Colorado have community policing projects like this. We don't, and that's a shame. Law enforcement shouldn't be strictly punitive."

"That's true," Hennessy mused.

She rushed ahead. "As for the budget concerns—"

"There are no budget concerns," Jonas said. "I can pay for the center."

She inclined her head. "Okay, then to get the community involved. I'd love to seek donations of building supplies from local businesses and renovate the space myself to save the city—and our benefactor—their money, whether it's necessary or not." Cagney shrugged. "I certainly have the renovation experience, and I think it's important to involve the residents of the Gulch as much as possible."

Murmurs filled the space.

"Just think how much local business donations will increase community investment in the place," she added.

Again, eager conversation ensued.

"Wait one damn minute," Chief barked, silencing everyone. "Officer Bishop, you are being insubordinate. It is not your place to waltz into a meeting to which you weren't invited and change your duty assignment on a whim."

"For goodness sake, Chief, stop being such an unreasonable taskmaster," the mayor said, spreading his arms. "I realize the young lady is your daughter and your employee, but she's what—thirty years old, Cagney?"

"Yes."

"Not to mention, she's making a generous offer and a professional sacrifice. There is no reason to accuse her of insubordination when she's showing the kind of community spirit that makes Troublesome Gulch a great place to live. You should be proud of Cagney instead of reprimanding her."

"She should receive a commendation," Hennessy added.

Cagney started to say that wasn't necessary, but—

"And considering the fact that we increased your budget so you could hire five new officers this year, surely you can spare one for this excellent cause," fired off one of the longest-standing, most respected city council members, looking over his half glasses at Chief. "Why is it we don't have any community policing projects in this town, Bill?" he asked.

The room hung in suspense.

Chief didn't bother answering the council member's question. Cagney knew he wasn't of the kiss-babies-and-hand-out-balloons school of law enforcement. "Fine. Open your youth center, but I'll assign an officer of my choosing," he said finally, struggling to hide his rage.

Cagney shook her head. "Sorry. That's unacceptable."

His hollow-point scowl shot toward her. "Excuse me?"

"If I loan out part of my property, I insist on being assigned to the project, as I'm sure you all understand. Plus, like I said, I have a great working relationship with the town's kids." She shrugged as though it didn't matter to her. "But if you don't want to take me up on my offer…"

"Oh, no. No," Walt Hennessy said quickly. "We definitely want to use the space."

Cagney spread her arms. "Then the officer assigned has to be yours truly. Simple as that." She angled her head at the mayor. "That is, if you, Walt and Chief approve."

"Oh, I approve wholeheartedly," Blackman said.

"I do, too. Your conditions are *perfectly* reasonable," said Hennessy pointedly, before lobbing the ball to Chief with a sardonic hike of one eyebrow.

Cagney bit the insides of her cheeks to keep from gloating. The mayor, city manager and the entire city council were actually ganging up on her father. She wanted to freeze this historic moment in her mind so she could replay it over and over whenever she needed cheering up. What could be better than seeing Chief backed against a wall?

The fact was, he couldn't say no to her near-perfect solution without revealing himself as an unreasonable, controlling dictator to the rest of them, and he was all about maintaining his image. For once, she'd kicked his personal agenda in the rear, and it felt great.

More than great. Vindicating.

The muscles in his jaw jumped, but finally he said, "Fine. I'll approve it against my better judgment."

"Thank you, sir," Cagney said, in as deferential a tone as she could manage while wanting to stick her tongue out at the guy and say, "nyah-nyah."

He father just glared.

One down, one to go.

She glanced toward Jonas. "So, what do you say, Mr. Eberhardt?"

"Oh, call me Jonas, please," he said, in a wry tone.

"Jonas, then. Will my space work for your purposes?"

Again. That wall, and he was just as backed against it as her father had been, if for different reasons.

His eyes narrowed as if he were trying to figure out exactly what she meant to prove by getting into the middle of this, but he maintained appearances. "It should work out just fine if the city approves. Thank you."

She played innocent. "Since you're spearheading the project, I assume you'll obtain the necessary permits? Or shall I?"

Jonas's hands were wound together on the tabletop. She noticed his knuckles whiten. "I'll get them."

"We'll make sure they're rushed through," the mayor said.

"Thank you." She tilted her head. "In fact, hey. I just had another great idea. Why don't you help me renovate, Jonas?" She threw him a one-hundred-watt smile. "It's your baby, after all."

"Oh, but it's your property."

"Still, I'd like to make sure it's exactly as you want it. I'll just follow your lead."

"I don't know if I'd call that a great idea," Chief said.

"Why not?" Hennessy asked.

Jonas eyed his nemesis stonily, and Cagney could see the tables turning. "Yes, why not? I'll be funding whatever the donations can't cover. Why wouldn't it be a good idea?"

Ha! Trapped another one, Cagney thought. Playing them against each other meant she came out the winner.

"Does that mean you're on board?" she asked Jonas.

He did a double take, apparently realizing what she'd just pulled off, then gave a barely perceptible nod of his head. "I'd be happy to do it. In fact, I insist. I'm here anyway, at least until the hospital wing is up and running."

"Then it's settled," the mayor said,

beaming. "It'll make a wonderful human interest story for the papers. Maybe even the Denver papers. Another feather in Troublesome Gulch's cap." He frowned, as if searching the annals of his brain. "Say, didn't you kids go to high school together?"

"That we did," Cagney said. "Graduated the same year. In fact, we were friends. Right, Jonas?"

"Right," he said slowly, as if trying to regain the upper hand in this game. Or at least get a grip on the rules of play.

"Though we'd lost touch over the years," she added.

"Excellent," the mayor said. "A heart-warming reunion, all for the good of the Gulch. What a story. I'll have my office put out a press release immediately." The city council members nodded in unison. "This is fantastic. Just splendid. I'm so glad you happened by, Cagney dear."

"Oh, believe me," Cagney said, feeling smug, "so am I." She clapped her palms together once and looked directly at Jonas. "So then. If you're free for coffee, we can head over to the Pinecone and do some brainstorming. I say, the sooner we get started, the better. Don't you think?"

Chapter Four

Jonas arrived at the Pinecone before she did and snagged a table toward the back. He ordered coffee for both of them, then waited. He had to admit, the bustle and chatter of the still-familiar diner felt like home. Twelve years gone, and he'd swear not a single decoration had changed, which was somehow comforting. The place even smelled exactly the same...like coffee and waffles and chicken-fried steak.

Still, he couldn't believe he'd let his ego rope him into close, personal proximity with Cagney for God knew how long. Months, at least. He could have handed off the renovation project to her, could've hired professionals out of his own pocket—any number of more palatable options. But no. The opportunity to enrage her father proved too large a temptation to pass up. What an impulsive idiot.

Despite himself, he had to hand it to Cagney. She'd pulled off one hell of a switcheroo in that meeting, smooth as silk, too. Begrudging admiration tugged at him. In all their teenage years, he'd never seen her stand up to her father once, at least not overtly. She'd always been more of an under-the-radar rebel. But the fact that she'd impressed him didn't mean he wanted to spend hours, days, weeks in close collaboration with her. What was that old saying…? Once bitten, twice shy? More like, once crushed, never again.

He felt too vulnerable around the woman.

On one hand, he looked forward to creating a safe space for Troublesome Gulch's teens. And, heck yeah, seeing that burst-a-vein anger on Chief's face had been a once-in-a-lifetime joy he wouldn't trade for anything. But working alongside Cagney?

Painful, on so many levels.

Not to mention dangerous.

Too late now.

Just then, the bell above the door jangled as Cagney entered. He sized her up as she wound her way through the seated customers, exchanging a word or a laugh here, a handshake there. She wore low-slung khaki cargo pants and an army-green tank top that perfectly set off her blond hair and offered a modest peek of her toned tummy. She looked strong and sexy. One hundred percent woman.

Not that he cared, of course. But he was man enough to acknowledge how attractive she was.

Finally, she arrived at their table, breathless and busy and eager to get started. Or maybe she was as nervous as he was dismayed by the whole fiasco. In any case, she began rambling immediately, even before she sat. "Hey. Oh—thanks for ordering. Anyway, I was running through stuff in my mind on the way over, and I don't think the permits are going to be a big deal because the place is already way up to code after my renovation of the rest, but—"

"Whoa. Slow down." He held up one palm.

"As much as I admire your sneaky coup in that meeting, we need to get a few things straight before we talk logistics."

She stilled, studying him, then sat. She shook her long, blond hair over one bare shoulder—which almost made him lose complete concentration—then anchored her elbows on the table. "Okay, ground rules. Fine. Ball's in your court, Jonas. Go for it."

"I know why you did this."

"Yeah? Why?" She wrapped her hands around the mug, lifting it to her lips for a sip.

"To make your father crazy."

A minismile lifted the corners of that luscious mouth. "That's part of it. A big, satisfying, yummy part, yes."

"What's the rest?"

She shrugged. "I like teenagers. I work well with them."

"Right." Totally unconvinced.

"Don't insult me by implying that I'm using the teenagers as a pawn in some mental chess game."

"You're not?"

She cocked her head, eyes wide. "You know better than anyone that I fit squarely into the category of teens who grew up in dysfunctional families, Jonas. What's worse was how disgustingly normal we Bishops looked on the outside." She huffed out a humorless laugh. "I walked through life feeling like a total imposter, which sucked. I'm sure I wasn't the only kid in that awful limbo position."

"Probably not, but I hardly think it compares to living in a beat-down trailer and eating food from a can most nights."

"I'm not discounting—" She broke off and uttered a frustrated sound. "This isn't a competition over who had the worst childhood, okay? You might not think I have a vested interest in the teenagers, but I deal with them on a regular basis, and I *get* them. I respect them. They know it, too."

He adjusted in his seat. Okay, she had a point. But that wasn't what he wanted to talk about. "Listen, you need to know up front, as much as I enjoyed seeing your dad pinned to the dartboard like that, I'm not happy about being tricked into the renovations—"

"So back out," she said, in a casually challenging tone. "Hire someone to replace you. I couldn't care less as long as the work gets done."

He hiked one eyebrow. "Is that so?"

"You might think this is some ploy. It isn't. This teen center is something I should've thought of long ago, but I didn't." She looked as if she were casting about for the right words. "It's hard to explain, but I feel alive for the first time in…forever, because of your idea, Jonas. So thank you for that, at least. Forgive me for assuming you had a more personal investment in the project than the financial backing aspect."

"I do." His irritation grew. "It's just—"

"You don't want to work with me," she said in a level tone, lowering her chin to pin him with a stare.

He tried not to react.

"It's okay. You can say it. It's not a news-flash. Your feelings came through loud and clear the other day."

After a moment, he expelled a breath. "It's complicated."

"In what way?"

He regarded her. "Don't be obtuse. There's a lot of baggage between us, Cag. It's an added layer of difficulty I hadn't anticipated. I'm as invested in the teen center as you are, if not more. But the situation is…awkward."

She considered that. "Okay, then let's make a deal. The teen center isn't about us. Agreed?"

"Agreed."

"So, when it comes to the project, we're all business. We'll leave our so-called sordid past out of it."

As if it were that easy. He could hardly watch her walk into a diner without being drowned in a wash of regret he'd never overcome and desire that would never be sated. "You can do that? Just…be all business?"

"I don't want to, but I can if I have no other choice."

He appreciated her straightforward attitude.

"Look, Jonas, you know all this, but apparently it bears repeating. I grew up in a family that never talked about anything important, and I think open communication is the way to go. Always." She gripped her mug with both hands. "But you did get railroaded into this, and if professional distance from me is what you need in order to get the project done—"

"Why did you become a cop of all things?" he blurted.

A strained pause ensued.

Finally, she ran her fingers through her hair. "God, it's a long story. Probably for later. Or for never, if you're serious about keeping this all business," she said pointedly.

"Just tell me."

A line of distress bisected her forehead. "Suffice it to say, I'd run out of options and my life was at a complete standstill. I was a mess after my friends died. After you—"

He dropped his gaze.

She inhaled through her nose, then blew it out her lips. "I skipped out on college—"

"Wait." His attention shot back up toward her face. "You didn't go to CSU?"

She shook her head sadly, her beautiful mouth quirked to the side. "Pathetic, I know, but I couldn't deal. Spent a year or so wallowing in clinical depression, doing nothing except feeling sorry for myself, suffering from crushing survivor's guilt and PTSD, missing my dead friends and watching way too much horrible daytime television."

Her gaze slid away, as if she were hiding something. "Then, the whole police thing just sort of fell in my lap. I didn't have work experience and had to make money somehow so I could move out. No other choices at the time. Good enough answer?"

He studied her, trying to ignore the pang of compassion he felt. The vague answer would do for now, but he knew it wasn't the full story. "Do you like it?"

A beat passed, but her expression didn't waver. "It pays the bills."

"Doesn't exactly sound like your life's passion."

"Not everyone is lucky enough to follow their passion. Now it's my turn to ask a question." She broke off momentarily, clearly anticipating his protests. When none came, she asked, "Why didn't you pursue writing like you'd planned?"

"How do you know I didn't?"

She bestowed her very best *duh* look, which was oh so familiar. "Because I know you. I still know you, as much as that probably irritates the hell out of you. And unless you're Stephen King, writing doesn't pay well enough to fund an entire wing of a hospital."

His nerves twanged. He didn't even try to deny it. "Mom got sick, and I was all she had. I had to earn money because she couldn't work and she needed medical care. Expensive medical care." A half shrug. "I just happened to have studied in a field that pays well."

He watched Cagney gulp. "So you went to college?"

"Yes."

She nodded slowly, and he could almost swear he saw envy etched into her expression.

"Where?"

"Seattle." He took a drink of coffee to buy time. "It was my senior year when the cancer showed up for the first time."

"I'm so sorry, Jonas. Ava was a sweet woman."

"I'm sorry, too." To his utter shock, he found himself overwhelmed with the urge to unburden himself to her like he used to. All those years of treatments followed by hope followed by the devastating news that the cancer had returned in some other part of his mother's slight body. All those years of wishing she had been emotionally stronger in her life, of vowing to be strong in his own in order to honor her legacy. And through it all, no one to talk to. But, he had to remember, Cagney Bishop wasn't his confidante.

"When did you lose her?"

He swallowed past the instant tightening of his throat. "Three months ago."

Her gaze softened. "Wow, so recently."

"It was a long haul."

"But it looks like you did a great job taking care of her. That has to offer some kind of solace."

"Care? I wasn't with her enough. I was always working. That's not taking care of someone," he said, his hands bunching into fists of their own volition. "Money's not everything, Cagney."

She raised her eyebrows. "Geez, Jonas, ease up on the defensiveness. I was giving you a compliment. I'm sure your mom felt cared for, whether you were out earning money to pay for medical expenses or home nursing her. It all matters."

He scoffed.

"Do you even know me anymore? You act like I'm a completely different person." Her eyes narrowed. "You think I don't know money's not everything? I'm a freakin' cop."

"Yeah," he sneered. "This from the woman who bought a fifteen-thousand-square-foot historic building."

"Yes," she said in a fierce tone. "An abandoned, crumbling building the city planned to tear down that I bought way under market, just to save a piece of history. And, not that you asked, but I purchased it with the insurance settlement money I received after the crash that changed my life completely and killed half my circle of friends. I carry a huge mortgage, too, so don't you dare accuse me of being materialistic."

A long uncomfortable pause stretched between them. He thought immediately about the heartless comments he'd tossed off the other day, and shame washed over him. He'd fostered a lot of anger over the years, no denying it, but deep down he wasn't that kind of person. He cleared his throat and met her gaze directly. "I meant to tell you…I'm sorry for what I said in the parking garage. About Tad. Your friends. I wasn't thinking straight and I lashed out. That's not how I usually operate."

Her shoulders dropped on a sigh. "You think I don't know that, Jonas?"

Not going there. "I'm truly sorry Mick and the others died. Truly. That's what I wanted to say."

Her eyes showed ravage, but they also shone with appreciation. "Apology accepted. Thank you. So," she said, breaking the tension, "can we call a truce, at least for the time being? We've got to get this project under way since it's my full-time job now, and if we butt heads through the whole process, Chief wins. Again." She allowed for the impact of that one word. "Besides, Troublesome Gulch needs a youth hangout. Badly. Hard as this may be for you to believe, today's Gulch teens are exponentially more bored than we were back in the day."

"Unimaginable, but okay," he said begrudgingly.

She blinked at him. "Okay? As in, truce okay?"

"I said it, didn't I?"

"Just checking," she said, holding up a palm. "God forbid I were to read into your words."

They both sipped their coffee.

After a moment, he huffed out something that could pass for a meager, monosyllabic laugh. "You torqued Chief off something good today in that meeting."

She flicked the notion away. "Eh, who cares about him? He was dead wrong to focus on his personal agendas or vendettas—whatever—rather than the good of the community. The whole room knew it. His resistance was all about you."

Jonas's gut contracted, but he managed to keep his tone light. "Still hates me, huh?"

She rolled her eyes. "He hates everyone.

No news there. Why do you think he has three unmarried daughters? Would you want that man walking you down the aisle?"

"Deirdre still with the FBI?"

Cagney nodded. "The L.A. field office."

"And Terri?"

"Couldn't tell you." Her eyes shadowed with sadness. "I haven't heard a single word from her since the day she booked it out of here."

Jonas reached over and squeezed her hand briefly, not missing the shock that registered in her expression. "I'm sorry about Terri. Still. It was…eye-opening to see you stand up to the old jerk finally."

Anguish darkened her gaze, which slid to the very old but highly polished wood floor. The fine smile lines around her eyes seemed to deepen. "Look, the last thing I want to talk about is my *father.* Now or ever."

"I share that sentiment."

"So, onward. What do you have in mind for the center?"

For the first time in more than a decade, Jonas felt a small lift of hope. If he guarded himself carefully, he just might be able to survive this. Sure, Cagney was a cop, but the more he talked to her, the more she seemed like the girl he'd loved back in the day and less like her father's shadow. Stronger, infinitely more sure of herself, but authentically Cagney nonetheless. Having a legitimate reason to hang out with her and not risk his heart again? Not such a bad proposition.

"I think we can do it pretty simply," he said, easing back in his chair. "Fun colors, big comfortable furniture. They have these giant bean-bag type things except softer and without the actual beans. They're called—"

"Foofs."

He pulled his chin back. "You know about Foofs?"

"I have a Foof in the bedroom. Most comfortable thing ever."

He didn't want to think about her bedroom. "Affordable and sturdy, and we can get them covered in a good, durable fabric. Something easy to clean. I think they'd be perfect."

"Agreed."

He nodded once. Done deal. "Then, I was thinking a computer section would be great, maybe, with Wi-Fi." He flicked one hand to the side. "I'll donate all that, of course. And we'll have parental blocks out the wazoo."

"Definitely. A computer section is a brilliant idea." She smiled. "I hadn't thought of that. It'll be a huge draw."

"And a necessary one. A lot of kids can't afford computers and yet their teachers require them to use them for homework. There are only so many available at the local library. It automatically puts the lower-income kids at a disadvantage." He shook his head with disgust. "What else?"

"Think fun."

"Okay. A big television for movie nights and such. Game tables, a karaoke stage. They just need a place to feel valued and wanted. A place to escape all the heaviness of…well, you know."

"Yeah," she said, her tone husky. "I definitely know." Her piercing blue eyes studied his face so long, he began to sweat beneath the scrutiny.

"What?"

"You're a good guy, Jonas. And you can't hide it."

"Who said I was trying to hide it?" He held up a finger. "However, businesslike. Your suggestion, remember?"

"Right." She pressed her lips together in mock seriousness. "Completely legitimate compliments are off limits in the corporate business world. How could I forget? I should be flogged immediately."

Suddenly, he felt tired. Bone-tired. Lifetime-of-mistakes-and-no-going-back tired. He wasn't in the mood to banter, because it would just make him want her more, which was impossible. "There's just no point, Cagney. It'll be easier for both of us if we acknowledge that and…move on."

She nodded, but he could tell her excitement dipped. Her face had always been a map of her feelings, except when she was around her father. Then she just went blank. "You're right." She took in a big breath. "Anyway, I'll use the police database to compile a list of at-risk youth so we can get the buzz started. Faith can help, too."

"Faith?"

"Mick Montesantos's little sister?"

He arched his eyebrows. "She's a grown-up?"

Cagney smirked. "Uh, yes. Hard to believe, I know, but we all age at the same rate. She's the counselor at the high school now, champion of disadvantaged kids far and wide."

"Wow." Guess he had been gone for a while.

She bounced forward in her seat, eyes shining. "Maybe we can send out invitations for a grand opening. Hey, I bet we can get all the printing and distribution donated. In fact—"

"Time out." He made a T with his hands. "Grand opening?" He shook his head. "We have months of hard work ahead of us before that happens if we want to do this thing right. There's the building itself, then screening and hiring staff and volunteers. One step at a time. You're getting way ahead of yourself."

"Yeah, I've been told it's one of my faults. I'm just psyched." She sipped her coffee, then glanced around for the waitress. When she caught the older woman's attention, she held her mug up and winked to request a refill.

The waitress glided over and topped both their cups. As she walked away, Cagney asked, "Ever get married, Jonas?"

The question caught him like a round-house kick to the chest. Inside, he reeled from it. It took him a moment to school his response into something that sounded flat. Disinterested. "No, I didn't. And you're getting personal again."

She inclined her head in apology.

More silence.

"Did you?" he asked, barely audible, hating

himself for the uncontrollable curiosity and the way he couldn't seem to breathe until he heard her answer. "I know you said you're unmarried now, but were you ever—?"

"Nope."

He gulped, ignoring the fact that one single word sent such intense relief through him, his limbs weakened. "Why not?"

She held up a finger. "I'd like it officially noted that you're getting personal here, too—"

"Forget I asked."

"Let me finish." She gave him a playful glare. "I was going to say, unlike you, I don't mind personal. In fact, I'm all about personal, so be quiet and let me answer. Unless you truly don't want to know." She paused, calling his bluff.

He couldn't make himself say a word.

Taking the cue, she said, "The thing is, I had my heart set on the perfect marriage. Soul mates, you know? The perfect life, a perfect family completely different from that mess I grew up in. A family where people talked and dreamed and respected one another. But that fantasy required the perfect partner."

"Never found him, eh?"

"Oh, I found him all right," she said, softly, staring into the steam of her freshly refilled coffee. She lifted one shoulder, then nailed him with a look. "But he left."

Chapter Five

As promised by Walt Hennessy, the permits came through at lightning speed, and Cagney and Jonas were off and running. Their personal mess faded to the background— they barely had time to breathe, much less butt heads. But they made no progress toward repairing their tattered relationship, either.

They'd spent two weeks scrubbing the space clean, then inspectors signed off on the electrical, plumbing and all those boring but important issues in record time. New girls' and boys' restrooms were framed and plumbed, the Sheetrock was hung, mudded and prepped for paint. They even had the bathroom fixtures installed, as well as a safe, serviceable kitchenette.

Within five weeks, all the rough stuff was finito.

Except when it came to their "relationship."

Such as it was.

Cagney had thought she'd get through to him at least a little by now, working side-by-side like they did, but he still treated her like a business associate—stubborn pain in the rear that he was. He showed up, discussed plans, paid bills, made things happen, yet shared nothing of himself. His remote treatment had begun to weigh on her and she couldn't stop obsessing about it. Maybe their time truly had passed. Maybe she should grow the hell up and stop pining for a man she'd never have again, a man who couldn't possibly make it more clear that he didn't want her anymore.

But she simply…couldn't.

The question nagged her…why *had* he really returned to the Gulch?

On the bright side, she had miraculously managed to avoid Chief so far in the process. If luck was on her side, he didn't want to deal with her any more than she did with him, and they could steer clear of each other until the end of time. Riiiight. She spent a lot of mental energy just waiting for the other shoe to drop where her father was concerned.

Nevertheless, she awoke early on Monday morning, day one of her favorite step in the process: decorating week. Jonas had pawned off a lot of the "girly jobs" to her with the lame excuse that he was splitting his time between the hospital project and the teen center. Whatever. In truth, she knew he had no interest in thumbing through paint chips and flooring samples, which was more than fine with her. Everyone knew men just got in the way when it came to all-important decor decisions.

But still, consumed as she was with the guy and everything they *weren't,* she knew she'd miss him this week. It wasn't as if she could call him up and chat to get her fix. It killed her that her feelings weren't reciprocated.

Not wanting to wallow in her abject loneliness any more than she already was, Cagney enlisted the help of Faith, self-proclaimed decorating guru, to select a color palette. Faith couldn't have been more thrilled to end her time off work on a high note. Her maternity leave had dovetailed seamlessly into summer break, which had begun at the end of May. However, June and July had flown by, and now that August had crept up on them, she was due back in school next Monday.

The kids wouldn't start the semester for another three weeks, but still. Faith had limited free time before real life intruded, and this was a great way for her to fill it. As the high-school counselor, she had a personal stake in making this center the best it could be, too, and she'd been pressing for it to be fully operational by the time school was in session. A lot of Faith's students—not to mention her and Brody's foster son— would be using the center if all went as planned.

Anyway, Cagney knew with her own art background and Faith's addiction to the home improvement channel on cable, the teen center could very well end up being a crowning jewel of Troublesome Gulch. Small consolation, considering the man who had gotten the ball rolling probably wouldn't even celebrate it with her, but oh, well. She couldn't bear to think about that right now. They had *tons* of work to do.

Little Mickie snoozed the late summer morning away as Cagney and Faith sat at a back table in the local hardware store perusing colors and textures, loving every minute of the process. The place smelled of fresh-cut lumber and mountain sunshine. Cagney loved the hardware store, her home away from home. It always reminded her of the loft renovation, the first true escape of her adult life.

They'd quickly decided on cork flooring because it would be easy to clean and it was an environmentally responsible option. Okay, it was also more chic than industrial linoleum. Rugs were a consideration for later—there was the whole cleaning issue they hadn't quite figured out. Right now, however, they needed to get those blank walls painted.

"What do you think of this?" Faith said, holding up a bright tangerine paint chip.

Cagney crinkled her nose. She loved the color, personally, but hoped to appeal to the masses. Tangerine might not do the job. "Wouldn't it limit our decorating options?"

Faith widened her eyes in mock horror. "Orange is the new black, Cagney. Don't be so suburban. Have you seen the average classroom?"

"Not lately."

"Well, it's psych-ward white." Faith pulled a bleh face. "These kids stumble out of school completely color-deprived and crazed for action. They need vibrancy and wildness and fun. That's what the teen center should embody."

Cagney laughed at Faith's theatrics. "Okay, you're the expert. Set it in the maybe pile. We'll think about doing an accent wall."

"Accent wall?" Faith frowned. "Stop playing it safe. I think we should go with all bright colors, a funky mishmash. Seriously. With the exposed brick and duct work, it would make the center look like a hip urban loft. The kids would go nutso for it. Trust me."

Cagney rolled that around in her brain. Faith had a valid point. "Okay, but let's keep our options open." They shuffled through many more colors, picking their favorites, dismissing the dull ones, laughing together over the hundreds of "shades" of whites and beiges, the perennial safe choices for the fearful masses.

White and beige, in all their permutations, were completely out of the question for the center—that they agreed on wholeheartedly.

After they'd amassed a giant pile of maybes, Faith pulled them closer so the culling process could begin. "Doesn't Jonas want a vote in the color scheme?" she asked, her tone breezy, as she studied and then set a beautiful jade chip in the finalists' pile.

Cagney paused a beat before answering. "Is that your not-so-subtle way of asking me how things are going between the two of us?"

Faith sighed. "Pretty much. I'd be a terrible poker player, huh?"

"Well, you'd be poor."

"So, spill," Faith said, leaning in. "How's it going?"

Cagney's heart felt like a jagged cinder block in her chest. "Not much to spill unfortunately. We're cordial and businesslike. Some days not even all that cordial, if he's in one of his moods. But always, always businesslike. Too businesslike." She blew out a breath and shoved her hair away from her face. "It's making me crazy. No matter how hard I try, I can't crack him. He's been back six weeks, Faith, and the only personal information I have about him came from that surfacey article in the newspaper."

Faith crinkled her nose. "They sure didn't give many details, did they?"

"He probably wanted it that way, closed off as he is. I don't even know his college major. Just that he did something in the computer industry."

"Which could be a lot of things," Faith said.

"Yes. I mean, what turned him from the Jonas I knew into this zillionaire philanthropist? He pushes me away if I even broach anything personal." Cagney spread her arms. "We *loved* each other. Shouldn't we at least be able to talk about stuff like college? Jobs? In detail?"

Faith jostled against her shoulder. "Aw, honey. He's obviously going through some major stuff, but he's still your Jonas. I can see it in his expression when he looks at you, plain as day."

Cagney rolled her eyes. "You're just a hopeless romantic who can't see that this situation isn't romantic in the least. It's just hopeless." She tossed aside a pathetic pastel paint chip that reminded her of elementary school cafeterias. How had *that* made it into the maybe pile? "Doesn't matter what I do. He won't talk about his life prereturn, and he absolutely won't discuss our past. Even though a single conversation could clear up so much of the strain between us."

"*Make* him talk."

Cagney shook her head. "If I push any harder, I guarantee he'll bail on Troublesome Gulch altogether. He's bitter, and he's got nothing keeping him here."

"Except the hospital wing. And the teen center."

"That won't do it. He can hire someone to oversee both projects if he wants to."

Faith pursed her lips, looking uncertain. "I'm not sure what to tell you. Give it time, I guess?"

Cagney huffed. "Oh, what, like another twelve years? I'm tired of waiting for my life to start."

"Cagney, you have a great life. Friends who love you."

"I know. That's not what I meant." She shrugged. "Forget it. I don't want to talk about it anymore. It's a lost cause."

"No cause is ever lost if you want it badly enough."

"If only that were true." Cagney dropped a wad of paint chips to the tabletop, leaned back and crossed her arms. "You know, initially I wanted us to pick up where we left off, rekindle the romance. But at this point, I just want his friendship back. We were friends before any of the rest of it, and I've missed that so much. If I could make that happen, I could be at peace with losing him as my lover."

"Really," Faith said, clearly dubious.

Cagney studiously avoided her friend's pointed stare. "Well…it's a step. It's something, and right now I have nothing. Give me a break."

"So, if you truly want to be friends with the guy, do friend things. Outside the confines of the teen center."

Cagney twisted her mouth to the side. "Can't. It's not part of our stupid deal. And I'm the idiot who suggested the deal in the first place."

"So? Deals change. You made the rules. Alter them."

Good point. But still… "I'm not sure he's ready."

"Are you?"

Cagney stared up at the exposed rafters and gave that some thought. "I don't know. Some days, yes. Others, no." She worried her fingers together in her lap. "The thing is, I've lost him once and it was the worst pain I've ever felt, Faith, next to losing Mick and the others. Going through that again, losing him and mourning him all over—" She shook her head at the mere thought.

"But what if you don't lose him?"

Cagney cast her a droll look. "Be realistic. He's made it more than obvious that he's way past done with me and everything we were. He hates my job—"

"As do you."

"He hates my father—"

"As do you."

"I wouldn't say I *hate* Chief," Cagney said, hoping she wasn't the kind of person to harbor such a horrible emotion in her heart and soul. "I just…don't like him. At all."

They both laughed.

Faith laid a hand over hers, and the two friends locked gazes. "Hon, what do you *want?* Bottom line."

Cagney didn't even have to think. Her desires had never wavered. "Jonas. I want him, the Jonas I once loved. I just don't know if he exists anymore, and yet I can't stop banging my head against that brick wall, hoping to break through." She bit the corner of her lip. "Glutton for punishment, huh?"

Faith, on the other hand, seemed infinitely more confident. "Well, as uncomfortable and scary as it is with him right now, if you want this, you've got to be the one to *make* it happen."

"I get that, but how? Without pushing him away?"

A long pause. "I don't know. I'd hoped it would be easier once you two spent time together, but it looks like he's going to fight you to the end. It doesn't matter, though. You're one of the strongest women I know."

Cagney gave an unladylike snort. "I am not."

"You *are.*" Faith spread her arms wide. "Look what you've sacrificed, what you've put up with over the years."

Cagney spread her arms wide. "Hello! My life is a textbook study in weakness. If I was the least bit strong, I would have told Chief to go to hell long ago, and I'd be an artist, not a cop."

"Not true. He hit you at a low point in your life and left you without a choice. I mean, 'Get out and make it on your own or become a police cadet'? What were you supposed to do? You'd just turned twenty and you were still grieving."

"I know. But I'm still *doing it,* and it's been years."

"And yet, despite the fact you don't love the job, you're a damn good cop, Cag."

"Who cares? I caved, under duress or not, and now I'm firmly in a rut."

"Well, there's plenty of time for a career change if you're really unhappy. Plus, you're already changing. You're working full-time at the teen center now, not pushing a radiator around the mean streets. That's a start."

"Right," Cagney said, her tone dubious.

"If anyone can do it, you can. You have mad survival skills, woman. I mean, you completely schemed Jonas into working with you on the center by using your father—his ultimate kryptonite—against him." Faith grinned. "Pitting the two of them against each other? Pure genius."

"True." Cagney chewed on that. "He had a vested interest in getting back at my father, and it worked for my purposes at that point. But I don't want him to be a part of my life for the same reason. If he doesn't want me— truly—then I'd rather savor what we once had and move on."

"What if that's not the case?"

A hopeful paused stretched between them.

"All collected evidence says otherwise."

"I disagree," Faith said, picking up another

stack of paint chips and aiming it at Cagney. "He'll deny it to his dying day, but we all know the truth. The whole reason Jonas Eberhardt returned to Troublesome Gulch was to seek revenge for some perceived wrong you inflicted upon him back in the day, even though he's mistaken about the whole thing, the big dummy."

"Totally."

"Well? People don't seek revenge against those they couldn't care less about. They just get over it."

"He told me flat out he didn't care, Faith. He couldn't have been more straightforward."

She laughed and shook her head. "Of course he said that, you goof. What else would he possibly say in his current mindset? 'You've been on my mind every single day for the past twelve years?'"

Cagney's cheeks heated. "Well, no. But—"

"He's a man. He has his annoying manly pride."

"Hate that stuff." Cagney pulled a face.

Faith nodded. "But it's fact. After the pain he suffered, losing you, he's not going to offer his heart up on a platter, just like that, and risk getting it broken again by his first love."

"I don't know that he ever loved me."

"Yes, you do."

A pause. "Okay, he *did*—past tense."

"He stayed in the Gulch, didn't he? He could've done that hospital press conference and hit the road for parts unknown. But he didn't. He's right here working with you." The two friends locked gazes. "That has to mean something beyond his desire to enrage your father."

Cagney knew what Faith was saying. She just hadn't a clue what to do about it. She truly feared coming on so strong that Jonas bolted. That cowardly part of her would rather always *wonder* about his feelings than confront head-on the ugly truth that he hated her.

Avoidance.

An unhealthy by-product of her childhood, she supposed.

But she was sick of talking about it.

They had a teen center to build.

"Fine, we'll see what happens." She snatched up the tangerine paint chip. "I like this after all, and the more I think about it, I love your idea about giving it an urban loft feel. Together with the plum and that fun acid green and the gorgeous deep jade." She picked up the chips, fanned them out and studied them, then turned them to face Faith. "They're wild, right? Polar opposites of psych-ward white?"

"That they are." Faith jabbed her an elbow. "Nice subject change, by the way."

Cagney eyed her and ignored the barb. "I meant to ask you. Do you know any talented, approachable taggers who might do some graffiti-style artwork on the back wall by the karaoke stage? I think that would be so cool."

"Do I know taggers?" Faith scoffed. "They're only in my office every other day, all school year long."

"Well—" Cagney smirked "—they're in mine, too, but I don't think they'd do me any favors after the zillion vandalism tickets I've written them."

"Good point," Faith said. She groaned. "I swear, I could open a spray paint store with all we've confiscated."

Cagney touched her arm. "Donate it to us instead. We can use all the donations we can get."

Faith's eyebrows raised. "Deal. Great idea."

"And recruit me some taggers. I want the best of them. The true artists, preferably with the smallest attitudes."

"Gotcha."

"We'd pay them, of course. As long as their designs are respectful and inclusive. No gang insignia, nothing inappropriate or personal, no ethnic or gender or other types of slurs. What I'm looking for is more of an urban anime feel. Fantasy. Graphic-novel-type stuff with a street edge."

"I'm your girl. Let me drum up some names and pull out the old faithful thumb-screws." Mickie started to fuss, and Faith lifted her from her nappy car seat. "Actually, thumbscrews won't be necessary. My little cache of taggers will be thrilled by the recognition of their talents *and* the money, mark my words."

Faith jostled Mickie, but the fussing increased in both volume and intensity. She cast an apologetic glance toward Cagney. "Is the color scheme set, then? I should go, before you know who goes into baby meltdown mode. It's about time for her daily wail."

"We're square. You go on."

As Faith stood to gather her baby gear, Cagney reached out and touched her best friend's forearm. "I hear you, Faith. Okay? About the Jonas issue, I mean. And...thank you for listening to me drone."

"You're welcome. I'm always here if you need to talk, and I'll be presumptuous and say that goes double for Erin or Lexy. We want to see you happy."

Cagney rolled her eyes, but in truth, the inclusiveness warmed her heart. "I'll figure something out."

"Oh, I have no doubt of that. Do me a favor, though, and keep me posted regularly so I don't have to drop those not-so-subtle hints you so love to point out."

Cagney laughed. "You got it."

Faith leaned down and kissed Cagney's cheek, and with that, mama and wailing baby were gone.

Cagney sat back, inhaling the fresh lumber scent. For the first time in weeks, she almost felt hopeful.

Chapter Six

So much for hopeful.

The animosity between her and Jonas on painting day reached epic levels within the first half hour, which had to be some kind of a record. He'd shown up grouchy, hadn't displayed the proper enthusiasm for the color scheme, if you asked her, and it had all plummeted downhill from there.

"You're absolutely sure these colors will be popular with the kids?" Jonas asked in a doubtful tone for about the tenth time since they'd begun painting four hours earlier.

They were doing three-foot horizontal

stripes around the massive room, except for the exposed brick and the graffiti wall backing the karaoke stage. The prep alone had been a monumental and tedious task; she didn't appreciate her artistic judgment being questioned repeatedly.

He never used to question her artistic choices.

You aren't an artist anymore, remember?

Cagney set her jaw as she bent down to dip her roller in the deep jade paint, second color up from the floor. "If you'd wanted a vote in the final paint colors, you were more than welcome to share your opinion instead of ducking out with a convenient excuse."

"I'm not doubting you, Cagney—"

"Yes, you are." She spun around and glared. "If you weren't, you wouldn't ask me the same question a thousand times. Geez!"

Jonas angled his head toward her. "Wow, someone woke up on the wrong side of the bed."

"Oh, really? You're one to talk." Her face flamed. "Like you care anyway. You wouldn't know the least thing about my bed," she muttered.

He gave her a quizzical look. "Excuse me?"

She gestured toward the ceiling. "We work every day right below my house, and you've shown zero interest in seeing the place I renovated with blood, sweat and tears over two solid years. My pride and joy. It was my whole world, and you couldn't care less." She flung her roller down onto the tray, splattering bits of jade paint on the drop cloth. "Some friendship we supposedly had. What a joke."

"But—"

"Oh, don't misunderstand me, I get it." She held both palms up toward him, feeling an uncontrollable rant coming on. "Loud and clear. No need to go over it again and again and again until my head explodes. We're not allowed to talk about beds or life or anything at all but this damn center, Jonas, are we? *I get it.* So, drop it. You told me to pick the paint without your input, and I picked the stupid paint." She turned away, hoping to return to the task at hand. "Live with it. Preferably in silence."

"Cag—"

She wheeled back. "Give it a rest! That rant? Yeah, that was femalespeak for leave me the hell alone, just FYI."

He just stood there, mouth hanging open.

Somehow that infuriated her even more. "Screw this. I'm going down the street for a cup of coffee," she grumbled, without waiting for him to answer. "I'm sick to freakin' death of all the males in my life thinking they get to make all the rules."

He caught her at the door and slipped his hand around her upper arm. "Hang on. I'm sorry. We started off on the wrong foot today."

"Ya think?" she said sarcastically, hanging her head and taking a few deep breaths.

"This is hard for me, too," he said.

"Yeah? Well, that's your choice." She turned toward him, gently shrugging her arm from his grasp. "It doesn't have to be this way. Don't you get it?"

He hesitated.

She could see the struggle in his eyes and took her chance. "We can't just pretend we never meant anything to each other. It's idiotic. I'm sick of talking about superficial crap all day, every day. I want to talk to *you*. About life. About things that matter. Like we used to." She laid a hand on his chest, shocked by the feel of the warm muscle beneath her palm and its instant impact on her insides. He still smelled the same, too, sort of citrusy-clean and leathery bad boy all at once. For one insane moment, she yearned to lay her face against his chest and breathe him in. "Either that or, I'm sorry, but I'd rather not talk at all. You have your conditions, and I have mine, too."

He surprised her. After a moment of silence, he reached up and tucked one long strand of hair behind her ear. It was the first time he'd touched her like that since his return, and she could scarcely draw air. The omnipresent pull of tamped-down attraction between them crackled to life, full and bold.

"Tell you what," he said, in that soothing voice she remembered from when they were teens and he'd tried to cheer her up after one of her many run-ins with Chief. "We've both been working way too hard, and we're under a lot of pressure from a million different directions."

"Understatement." She huffed. But she was already starting to feel better, and just because he tucked her hair behind her ear and used The Tone. Pathetic.

"Before this goes any further downhill, how about I go get us both coffee, my treat, and then we'll take a nice, relaxing break. Regroup." He paused. "Talk."

She almost didn't want to believe it. "You mean, *talk* talk? About real life?"

He gave a single, jerky nod. "Sure. A short talk, though. We have tons of work left to do."

The smile she gave him felt tremulous, probably because she suddenly wanted to cry. She gulped the emotion back. "Okay, then. If you're serious." She took her palm from his chest, even though she didn't want to. "I like my coffee—"

"I know how you like your coffee, Cag," he said, in a droll tone. And with that, he left.

Alone, she smiled, hugging her arms around her middle.

He knew how she took her coffee.

And they were going to *talk*.

God, she was pathetically easy. Then again, so what?

Buoyed with hope, Cagney practically danced to the middle of the room, then laid down flat on her back with her knees propped up. The drop cloth softened the floor a little. She stared at the exposed ductwork, gorgeous since they'd paid to have it cleaned until it gleamed. Though some days it seemed as if they'd never finish, the place really *was* coming together bit by bit.

She'd always hoped to turn this level of her home into an artist's studio one day, which was why she'd never done anything to it in the first place. But this was even better because she and Jonas were building something together. And who knew? Maybe she could give some art lessons to the kids. The teen center was supposed to serve as a kind of segue or adjunct to the art therapy wing at the hospital, after all.

Warmth spread through her just thinking about it, and she grinned. She was actually working with Jonas. And he'd gone to get her coffee. Okay, maybe there was the teensiest glimmer of hope for them. Wouldn't that be amazing? Perfect. Fairy tale romance kind of stuff, really.

Her mind on that track, she closed her eyes and indulged in a mental picture of the two of them making hard, passionate love right here in the middle of the redecorating mess. She'd wanted him for so long, she couldn't help herself. The cloth-covered cork floor against her back, years of pent-up need leaving her dizzy with every imagined deep thrust. She pictured her hands on his back, which would be every bit as muscular as his chest had been, but this time, the two of them would be skin on skin. Just as it should be.

She'd always loved the scent of his skin.

How decadent to lie here and indulge in this illicit fantasy, but why shouldn't she? In fact, if only she could convince him of how right it could be between them, they might as well go ahead and live it out. They were grown adults. All the windows were masked with brown paper for the painting process. It's not like any passersby would catch them.

Then again, she'd always been a closet thrill seeker. Knowing that they could be caught by some random Gulcher would only increase the excitement if you asked her....

Her nerve endings throbbed from the mere thought of it when she heard the door open. "That was fast," she said, sitting up slowly and bracing her elbows behind her.

Immediately, the fantasy iced over and she scrambled to her feet. "Chief." Her heart thudded, almost as if he'd caught her doing exactly what she'd been imagining. As if he could invade her thoughts as easily and unapologetically as he'd riffled through her belongs way back when. Her flesh flamed. "I didn't know you were stopping by today." So much for her unbroken record of avoiding him since that fateful meeting at the city building.

Her father, grim-faced as ever, loomed in the doorway. Broad-shouldered and fists clenched, he looked around the place as if it were a flophouse rather than an incredible, hopeful space. The man had the power to put a damper on just about anything. "This is what you're drawing a police officer salary for? Lying on the floor in the middle of the day?"

Not a single kind word before he launched into her, but she was damned sick of it. *Game on.* She crossed her arms protectively across her middle. "If you must know, we've been working since six this morning, and I continue long into the night, every night." As if she owed him an explanation. "You have no right to question my work ethic."

"I'll question anything I damn well please." He puffed his chest out. "You still work for me. Answer my question."

Argh, that rankled. "We're taking a coffee break."

He made a big sarcastic show of glancing around the space. "I don't see any coffee."

She toyed with ignoring the comment, but like the man said, he was still at the top of her chain of command. She couldn't dismiss accountability completely. "Jonas went to get it," she said grudgingly.

"Oh, Jonas went to get it," he mocked, stalking around the place inspecting the walls. "Isn't that sweet. What the hell kind of acid-trip colors are these?"

Anger flashed through her, and she didn't want to revert back to childhood survival mode and stuff it down. Not anymore. Somehow having this project made her feel stronger than ever, especially knowing how much the town was behind her. "Colors intended to appeal to the clientele," she snapped. "It's a teen center, not a prison, and how it's decorated is up to me. What do you want, Chief?"

He spun to face her, eyes narrowing. "What do you mean, what do I want? This establishment is in my jurisdiction. I can walk in here any time I please."

She hiked her chin. "It's still my home."

His body tensed with anger. "Not since you waltzed into that meeting uninvited and humiliated me both as a daughter and an employee by offering it to the city."

So, that's what all this was about. Should've seen it coming. "I didn't humiliate you. You did that to yourself. You were wrong, not that you'll ever admit it."

"Watch your mouth."

She ignored the ominous tone threaded through those three little words and held on to her indignation. "I won't watch my mouth. If you're going to barge in uninvited and criticize all the hard work I've been doing, I'll say what I please. Ever heard of positive reinforcement? It's a management style that works quite well. You should read up on it."

For a moment, time froze.

"See, this is the problem." He started walking again, waggling his finger in a way that managed to seem languid and threatening at once. "This right here."

She glanced around, her irritation blooming. "What are you talking about?"

"You hook up with that kid again, and suddenly you're back to being disrespectful. Willful."

She planted her fists on her hips. "Perhaps it escaped your notice, but I'm thirty years old, and so is Jonas. We're hardly *kids,* and we're certainly not 'hooking up.' If anyone's being disrespectful, it's you."

His eyes glittered like knife blades. "Respect is earned, Cagney."

"How ironic to hear that coming from your mouth," she said with disgust, picking

up her roller, just to have something to
hold. "And if you'd ever be truthful with
yourself about my high-school years, not
that I'm holding my breath, you'd admit I
was never disrespectful or willful back
then. I wish I had been more like Terri.
Instead, I was your meek little puppet,
Chief, something I regret with my whole
soul. But I'm not that weak girl anymore,
which has nothing to do with Jonas. It's all
me. *Just me,*" she said, echoing what she'd
told him so many years ago.

"I never should've let you buy this place,"
he growled, his gaze sliding over her as if she
were some worthless piece of trash. "You
have all kinds of crazy ideas now about
who's in charge."

"I'm in charge," she snapped. "It's *my* life,
and you couldn't have stopped me from
buying this place if you'd tried. I can spend
my money however I like." Her voice rose of
its own volition. "I'm not your property and
I never asked you for a thing."

He laughed. Cruelly. "You forget, the only
reason you had that money was because you
defied me."

Confused, she frowned. "What?"

"If you hadn't, you never would've been

in that SUV on prom night with your so-called friends, drinking alcohol you stole from our house."

She couldn't believe he still held a grudge after all these years. Most of the parents had pulled their children closer. Not Chief.

Anger roiled in her gut. "Exactly. I would have been with Jonas. *Safe.*"

He snorted. "Probably with your prom dress hiked up around your waist, too. That's what boys like him want."

Her stomach lurched. "You make me sick. You have no idea what my relationship with Jonas was about."

"Argue all you want, but I did the right thing." He glared. "You brought that whole prom night fiasco on yourselves, and you killed poor, innocent Tad Rivers for no reason but your own selfishness. Live with *that.*"

Pain and rage exploded through her, leaving her hands shaking and her heart slamming against her ribs. She could hardly see straight. Did he think she wasn't living with it? Every day of her miserable life? The last thing she needed was more guilt trips or blame, especially from him.

"You killed him, I didn't!" she yelled,

unable to keep her voice from shaking. "You forced me to go with him."

"Did I force you to drink and drive? To break the law?"

"You'd have been happier if I'd died in that crash, just to prove some twisted point of yours. Don't think I don't know that." She pointed the roller toward the door. "Get the hell out of my house! You're not welcome here!"

"Watch your damn mouth," he yelled, stomping forward until they were faced off.

He'd crossed a line this time, and if he thought she was going to cower or tamp down her feelings, he was sadly mistaken. "Go to hell! And get out, unless you're planning on hitting me," she goaded, almost hoping he would. "In that case, bring it on. Please. I'd love for that scandal to ripple through your precious department."

"I've had enough of your smart mouth."

"Then leave," she yelled, her whole body shaking. "You're interrupting my workday. I mean it, Chief! Speaking as your daughter. Leave!"

Jonas heard the disturbance from down the street and started running. He burst through the door, ready to throw aside the tray holding two coffee cups and a bakery bag if need be. His brain blared with alarm, and his chest heaved.

He screeched to a halt and looked from Cagney to none other than her father, then back. "What's going on? The whole street can hear you two screaming at each other."

"Look what the cat dragged in," sneered Chief.

Jonas ignored him, focusing on Cagney. "Are you hurt?"

She shook her head, but her chin quivered, and she looked distant and ravaged.

"Don't you dare imply I'd hurt my daughter."

"Imply it?" Jonas sneered, showing zero signs of intimidation. "I know you'd hurt her, and you'd sleep like a baby afterward, you power-hungry bas—"

"Jonas, it's okay," Cagney said, her voice cracking. She cleared her throat. "He was just leaving."

"I never said I was going anywhere," Chief said.

Jonas studied her a moment longer, convinced Chief had done or said something beyond horrible, then straightened up and held the door open. He set his jaw. "You heard the lady. Time for you to leave, Bill. We have work to do."

Chief stepped closer to him, glancing up. "And if I don't? Who you gonna call? The cops?" He chuckled at his own weak joke, but his anger because Jonas deigned to use his first name rather than his title came through clearly.

"You know," Jonas said coolly, "a man with true power doesn't have to shove it down other people's throats."

Unused to being defied, Chief's face purpled with rage. "Yeah? Well a real man doesn't return to a town he was never welcome in the first place, either."

"Chief, stop it!" Cagney said. "Jonas, don't listen to a word he says."

"Get out, you twisted bastard," Jonas growled. "Your mind games can't hurt me anymore, and I think you've tortured your own daughter enough for a lifetime."

Chief sauntered past him, stopping at the threshold to glare pointedly back at Cagney. "Don't forget what I said."

Jonas shut and locked the door behind him, then set the coffee tray on the floor. He crossed to Cagney in three long strides, stooping down to cup her elbows and peer into her face. "What did he say to you? Are you okay?"

Clearly she wasn't. Not at all. Her face had paled, and her gaze remained distant and pained. She looked shaky; sweat beaded her upper lip. It went completely against their agreement, but without saying a word, he pulled her against his chest and wrapped his arms around her. She buried her face and burst into tears.

He did the only thing a decent man would do in this situation—he held her tightly, rubbed her back, rocked her as her body racked with sobs seemingly from the depths of her soul. He tried not to inhale the alluring pear-and-vanilla scent of her hair, to notice how perfectly her warm curves molded against his lean angles. They'd both grown up, filled out, become adults, and yet they still fit together like two halves of a friendship medallion.

God, how amazing to hold Cagney again. Too good.

Too right.

Too impossible.

"He accused me of killing 'poor, innocent Tad' with my selfishness. Like I don't already feel guilty enough?"

Jonas closed his eyes, centered himself in the here and now as best he could with slow, deep breaths. "Shh, it's over. Just let it go, Cag. He's gone."

"He's never gone," she said, her voice clogged and watery. "Don't you see? That's the problem. My life is utter hell because of him."

He felt her bunch the back of his shirt in her fists.

"I'm thirty freaking years old, Jonas. It's ridiculous and embarrassing that I'm still squirming under his thumb."

"Which begs the question, why are you?"

She huffed out a completely unamused laugh, her breath warming his skin through his shirt. "Because I set my own trap, which probably thrills him to no end. He's my boss. I have a mortgage now, responsibilities. And I don't exactly have any other marketable skills or an education," she said with a razor edge of bitterness. "Believe me, he's not a part of my life other than workwise. I cut him off long ago, which of course means I don't get to see my mom much," she added sadly, "but that's the price I had to pay."

He pondered that a moment. "Sure seems like he's still managing to make your life crazy beyond the workplace."

"Yeah, well, you know him. He's a control freak. He insinuates himself into my world as much as he possibly can, tries to control me. That's his MO, same as always."

What a nightmare. "Have you ever considered leaving Troublesome Gulch? It worked like a charm for me."

"Leave and do what? Enroll in college as a thirty-year-old freshman? Start over as a rookie in some other police department where I don't know anyone? No seniority, no ties to the community? The thought makes me physically sick. No." She shook her head against his chest. "The Gulch is my home. My friends are here, my loft, which I love."

"And your father, who makes you crazy."

"Why should I let him drive me away from a town I adore like he did Terri? Besides, Troublesome Gulch can't be all bad. You came back after all these years, didn't you?"

She had a point. If only she knew why he'd come back in the first place. Guilt sprayed through him like buckshot.

He toughed it out. "What can I do?"

She half hiccupped, half sobbed as she slowly relaxed. "Just hold me. Please. I know you hate me, but—"

"I don't *hate* you. It's just…complicated."

"I'm tired of complicated, Jonas. I'm tired of games and fear and remorse and regrets. I'm tired of watching my every move, of trying to figure out Chief's next move so I can stay ahead of him. Departmental politics. City politics. Personal politics. You-and-me politics. I'm sick and tired of it all."

"I understand."

"My life wasn't supposed to be this way. *We* weren't supposed to be this way."

"This isn't about us right now."

She laughed bitterly at the irony of that statement. "Right. My whole life is about us. What we were, what we aren't anymore. That's what you don't get. Everything's spinning out of control, and I have no clue how to slow it down, much less stop it. I'm so…exhausted from trying to make things right."

"So stop trying."

"I…I don't know how."

For several long moments, he just rocked her. He ran his fingers through her silky hair, because he couldn't help himself, then rested his cheek on the top of her head. He wasn't great at this sympathy stuff, but he had to take a stab at it. "My mom, you know, she had her problems, but she was a good woman. She lived through a lot of hard times."

Cagney sniffled. "I know."

"When things got really bad for me, she used to say, 'Memories are made up of a whole string of nows.'"

"That sounds like Ava."

"Yeah. It used to annoy me, because my 'nows' sucked so much. But I finally figured out it was her way of telling me to keep my mind on all the small bits of good in life, even when it didn't seem like there were any." He smiled sadly. "There always were, when I dug deep enough."

"She was pretty darn smart, that Ava."

Jonas sighed. "Wish I'd taken her advice more often."

"You're lucky," Cagney said, her voice calmer. "My mom's okay. I love her, but I don't respect her, and it kills me to admit that."

Jonas hugged her tighter.

"She lets Chief run her world to this day, and I can't imagine that she's happy. The only advice she ever managed to give me was, 'Just try not to anger your father.'" Cagney scoffed. "She's such an enabler in the whole unhealthy mess."

"I'm sure she did her best." Jonas could see Cagney's side of it, though. "I guess my point with the Ava story is, don't let Chief's twisted issues tarnish your memories of the teen center by ruining the 'nows.' We're doing a good thing here, Cagney, despite a few bumps. Focus on that."

"Yeah, right." She sniffled. "Few bumps. You hate the paint Faith and I picked."

"No, I don't. It's just…wild."

"Kids *like* wild."

"I know. You're one hundred percent right. I was thinking like a thirty-year-old businessman, not a fifteen-year-old skater boy. I'm sorry."

She paused, peering up. "Did you just say I was right?"

He laughed softly. "I said one hundred percent right. I also said I was sorry."

Another pause. "Okay."

He set her apart from his body gently, rubbing her upper arms. "How about some coffee, hmm? I brought you a cranberry white chocolate scone, too. You still like those, right?"

"Who wouldn't like them?" She smeared at her tears with the backs of her hands. As he turned toward the coffee tray he'd abandoned by the door, she reached out and touched him. "Jonas."

He glanced back.

"Thanks. I'm sorry, too. For the…" She gestured to the space between them. "I promised we wouldn't get pers—"

"Don't sweat it. I know how toxic your father is, Cag, the kind of havoc he can wreak. Everyone needs a hug now and then. Besides, I was the one to break the rule, not you."

"So we're okay?"

"We're okay." He gestured toward a neatly folded stack of extra drop cloths in one corner. "Grab some of those and wad them up so we'll have something comfortable to sit on."

"Okay, but—" She clamped her bottom lip between her teeth, looking unsure.

"But what?"

"We could go up to my place," she suggested, softly, watching him through her spiky, wet, chestnut-brown lashes. "Real furniture. Great view. Excellent renovation job."

Part of him wanted to. Badly. But that warning siren in his head told him succumbing to his weakness for her during an emotional moment would be a devastating choice for both of them.

The physical attraction between them was

alive and well, snapping with electricity. That wasn't the problem. Despite it, he hadn't gotten to the point where risking his heart with her again seemed like a wise choice, no matter how enticing the idea of letting his guard down seemed. But neither of them needed another heavy conversation at the moment.

"Down here's fine," he said lightly, bending to pick up their refreshments. He turned back and winked at her. "I want to bask in the cool colors."

They sat on the floor across from each other, with five thousand square feet of partially painted space around them, and yet it felt intimate to Cagney. They'd jumped some sort of an emotional hurdle—thanks to Chief, ironically—and she didn't want to lose any of the momentum.

Truthfully, she hadn't expected him to go up to her place, but like Faith had advised, she needed to work for this. She'd lived cautiously for way too long. If she never threw the offers out there, he could never take her up on them. It had been a long shot and hadn't paid off.

This time.

But at least they were sharing a moment,

a scone and a semblance of solidarity, which was more than they'd done since his return.

She bit into the scone and made a yummy sound. After she'd swallowed and sipped her coffee, she decided it was time to delve into Jonas's life beyond this youth center. The hug had emboldened her. Just talking, right? How hard could it be? They had to start somewhere, and she'd stick to the totally safe topics. "Did you like living in Seattle?"

"Yeah. It's great there, the Pacific Northwest. Green. Misty. Clean." He hiked one shoulder. "The people are nice. Laid-back."

She nodded. "I've never been there." She'd never been anywhere, she realized, with a pang of yearning. "So I take it you studied computers in college."

"Yes."

"Very practical of you," she said, halfway teasing.

"It's a pretty creative field if you want it to be."

She nodded again, not so sure about that, but what did she know? Her college dreams had gone up in smoke. Literally. "What exactly did you do for a living?" She watched him closely for cues she was getting too personal, but he still seemed open, relaxed despite her questions.

He took a drink of his coffee. "Did programming for a while, then one of those infamous big layoffs hit the company I worked for during the dotcom crash, and I got swept up in it with all the rest."

"Wow, I'm sorry."

"Don't be. It was the best thing that ever happened to my career."

"How so? If you don't mind me asking."

He ran his fingers through his hair. "A friend from college and I used the downtime to design a search engine application that took off."

They hadn't mentioned that *in the newspaper article.* But why was she surprised? Their small-town newspaper, much as she loved it, never failed to mention the quirky "news" bits, but she didn't expect Harrison, the grizzled old features reporter, to boot up the Internet and do a little background poking. Not his style. "A search engine? Really? Which one?"

He named it, remaining totally calm as her eyes bugged.

"Holy—" Jonas hadn't just succeeded, he'd blown the roof off of his chosen profession. Certainly Harrison could've unearthed *that* nugget. She braced her palms on the floor in front of her crossed knees and leaned forward. "You're kidding me! You created that?"

"Yep."

"But—how?"

He raised his eyebrows. "Trial and error. Lots of work."

"Jonas, that's huge, and you're so casual about it." She shook her head, stunned. "I mean, that's like Google but not Google."

"We were pre-Google." He reached over and broke off a small bit of her scone, then stared off in the distance. "When our stock went public, it split and split and split— beyond our wildest dreams, really. We ended up selling after a few years for…well, more than we'd ever imagined."

"That's amazing." She knew she was beaming at him but couldn't stop. "You probably never have to work again," she said, without really thinking and just because she'd love to have the luxury of being able to tell Chief to piss off.

"Everybody has to work in one way or the other." He looked uncomfortable all of a sudden. "Philanthropy is my thing now."

Worry niggled at her mind when she heard

his underlying defensiveness. She tried to steer things back onto the positive path. "Oh, I know philanthropy is work. That's not what I meant. You have a lot of options is all. More than the average Joe, probably. Wow. At age thirty, too." Her chest expanded until it felt near to busting with pride for all he'd accomplished. "You're one of those success stories we regular folks read about in *Time* and *Fortune*."

He glanced away, his smile completely gone.

Why was he disengaging? What was she doing wrong?

"Jonas? Are you okay?"

"I'm one of those regular folks, Cagney. It all fell into place for me through hard work, that's all."

Was he uncomfortable with the spotlight? He didn't have any reason to be. "Now's not the time for self-deprecation."

"I deserved a bit of good karma in my life. At least, that's what I told myself."

"You did. You totally did." Her voice sounded overly chipper in her own ears, as if she were trying to hold on to their sense of ease, though she already felt it slipping through her fingers. "Why didn't you tell me sooner?"

"Why?" He eyed her warily. "Does it matter?"

Taken aback, she blinked a couple times. How had this light conversation gotten so offtrack, so quickly? "Well, no, it doesn't *matter*. But it's incredibly exciting, something you share with those you—" She pressed her lips together, remembering that he *didn't* love her. "You should be really proud is what I'm saying. That's *all* I'm saying."

"I'm used to it. It's just my life."

Fine, but it was new and exciting to her and she wanted to hear more about it, to live vicariously through him. She didn't know anyone else who'd gone beyond the ordinary to make such a huge contribution to the world. Somebody from Troublesome Gulch, no less.

The boy her father had said would amount to nothing.

She laughed suddenly at that thought, clapping her hands together.

"What's funny?"

"Just imagine what Chief thinks about all this."

His expression darkened to something just this side of anger, and she knew instantly she'd said the wrong thing. Her heart lurched.

"I have zero interest in impressing your father, Cagney, if that's what this is about."

She froze, thrown off by the harshness of his reply. "*This* isn't about anything." Her airway tightened. "You think I give a rip about impressing Chief? Really? After the conversation we just had?"

"Sure sounded like it."

"But—that's not at all what I meant."

He drained the rest of his coffee and crumpled the cup in his hand. "Frankly, if I wasn't good enough for that judgmental bastard, or any of these Gulchers, when I lived in a trailer, I sure as hell don't care what any of them—or you—think now that I could buy and sell his whole town."

"Jonas—" Confused, Cagney rested her head in her spread, shaky fingertips. "You're taking my words completely out of context. You were *always* good enough. Too good for me, if you want the truth."

"Right." He stood then, closed off as ever.

All the progress they'd made fizzled right before her eyes, and she had no idea why or how it happened. Hadn't she been complimenting him? Congratulating him? The man had one hell of a large chip on his shoulder, not that she could blame him. But still. Didn't he know her at all? "I'm sorry. I didn't mean to—"

"Dead topic, and I don't want your apology. Let's just get back to painting."

The coffee soured in her stomach. She stood, floundering, feeling helpless and hating it. "Look, if I said something to offend you—"

"You didn't. Let it go," he said, his tone clipped in a way that told her he wasn't being honest. "I have to be at the hospital later this afternoon. I don't want to leave the paint job half-done."

Frustration set in. She was trying so hard, but this subtext beneath implication beneath innuendo made her stomach hurt. It smacked of her childhood, and she didn't like it one bit. Whatever happened to the concept of open, direct communication? She whipped her arms open wide. "You know, I can always call in reinforcements if you're stretched too thin."

He narrowed his gaze.

"This center and everything it represents?" She pressed a fist to her chest. "I'm all-in, Jonas. And I have plenty of friends who would help me paint and furnish, whatever else it requires. You need off the hook, just say the word. I know you only agreed to help to piss Chief off anyway."

He blew out a breath, peered up at the ceiling. "I'm perfectly capable of handling my commitments without your help, okay? Let's just get it over with."

The teen center project wasn't supposed to be about "getting it over with." She watched him stalk over to the plum-colored paint, which was the stripe at ceiling level. He dipped his roller, climbed the stepladder and went at it with a vengeance, ignoring her completely, like he had in the first weeks of the project. It was as if she wasn't in the room at all, which he probably would've preferred.

Well, two could play at that game.

Then again…she didn't want to play games. Not with Jonas.

Lost, confused, she stumbled back to her own paint tray. Tears stung at her eyes, and she didn't even try to hold them back. It's not as if Jonas would look at her again today anyway. Letting them fall would at least ease her own tension and pain.

Un-freaking-believable.

One conversation gone awry, and just like that, they were back to square one. They couldn't even communicate through one simple topic. Yet another piece of evidence that their chance for true love had long since passed.

Chapter Seven

This knee-jerk thing with him *had* to stop.

He couldn't keep taking things out on Cagney. It wasn't fair, and it wasn't the kind of guy he wanted to be. She just got under his skin in a way no one else ever had, which made him lose his cool far too often.

Excuses, excuses.

Jonas sat on the balcony of his hotel suite in Crested Butte, one foot propped on the railing. The sun was about to set in spectacular fashion, but he couldn't stop castigating himself long enough to enjoy the view. Instead, he took a pull from his beer and settled in for a world-class brood. God, he'd left her there crying, for Pete's sake, as if he were some kind of unfeeling beast. Crying and alone in the middle of an empty warehouse, and he pretended not to have noticed, all because he wasn't sure how to begin the apology. Just like the cold-hearted bastard she'd accused him of becoming, and he couldn't even deny it.

Damn it.

She'd simply been excited for all he'd accomplished.

He knew that now, in hindsight.

And yet, thanks to his stupid pride, he'd done jack to set things straight between them. He kept trying to convince himself he was a better man than her father, but his actions repeatedly told a whole different story. His grip on the beer bottle tightened.

You've become just like him. How could you let him win?

Her words sliced through his brain again, and he closed his eyes to shut them out. It didn't work; it just made the words reverberate louder inside his head.

This dysfunctional, neverending cycle of wary closeness followed by misunderstanding, lashing out and finally regret had to stop.

Now. It was up to him to end it, but he didn't know how. He wasn't good at relationships. Not enough practice, he supposed, and definitely not enough role models. All he knew was, he didn't want to perpetuate that kind of life, especially not with Cagney. She'd survived enough turmoil.

Hadn't they both?

He stared out at the mountain vista and felt utterly, painfully alone. Lonely. He didn't have his mother anymore, no family at all.

No one.

Whoopee.

He had nothing but a massive bank account and an even larger roster of regrets. And the worst part? Nobody to blame but himself.

The ring of his cell phone jolted him from his sulk, and he pulled it from the clip on his belt. Probably Cagney, and if it was her, he would apologize immediately. Turn over a new leaf. Start fresh.

"Jonas here," he said, after snapping it open.

"Jonas Dagnamit Eberhardt, as I live and breathe," came the thick Jersey twang of his best friend and search engine cocreator, Tony Petronelli. "It's five o'clock somewhere, bro. Why so businesslike?"

Despite his foul mood, Jonas smiled. It had been way too long since he and Tony had talked, and man, it felt good to hear a friendly voice. "Hey, I've got a beer in my hand. Deep into a couple of projects is all. You know how I get."

Tony grunted with disapproval. "You work too damn much. Wanna know how I spent the day?"

"Lay it on me."

"Deep-sea fishing in the Caribbean. Now *that's* a life."

"Catch anything?"

"Not a damn thing, and I couldn't care less."

Jonas laughed. "How the heck are you, Tony? Where are you, for that matter?"

"Antigua," he said. "Sun, sand, the ocean and a beautiful woman by my side on the yacht. What more can a man ask for?"

What indeed? A pang of envy struck Jonas.

"Can I assume the beautiful woman is Kelli?" he asked, referring to Tony's long-time girlfriend. "Because otherwise I might have to fly out there and kick your ass."

"You betcha, it's my Kelli. That's why I'm calling."

"Sorry?"

"We're getting married!" Jonas heard Kelli yell from the background, punctuating the announcement with her infectious, bubbly laugh.

"That's right," Tony said, sounding proud. "I popped the big Q, and she actually said yes. Blew my mind. Guess my homely-Tony's-a-good-bet propaganda campaign over the years actually worked. Who knew?"

"Boy, that's no lie." Tension seeped from Jonas's muscles just hearing the elation in his friends' voices. He couldn't deny the swirl of jealousy in his heart, either. "Congratulations, buddy. I mean it. Kelli is a fantastic, top-shelf woman, and you totally don't deserve her," he joked, holding his beer up in a long distance toast before taking a swig. "Excellent catch."

"Thank you, thank you."

"Has she caught on yet to the fact that her married name is going to be Kelli Petronelli?" Jonas asked. "That might just be a deal breaker."

"She did. She's actually thinking of hyphenating."

"Kelli MacNamara-Petronelli?" Jonas pulled a face. "How's that an improvement?"

Tony laughed, robust and full. "That's what I keep telling her. Better to sound like a stripper from Atlantic City than have a name with twenty-four letters in it—ow!"

"She hit you?"

"Yup."

"Smart woman. Put her on."

There was some phone shuffling, then Kelli's breathy voice said, "Jonas. Sweetie, we miss you so much! Drop what you're doing this instant and fly to Antigua to celebrate with us. The weather is perfect, and the new yacht is beautiful."

Yearning tugged at Jonas. Why didn't he feel that he deserved that kind of a carefree life? Hadn't he earned the right to ease up? If only his whole world hadn't centered on revenge for the past twelve years...

"I miss you guys, too. Wish I could, but I'm in the middle of a couple of big projects."

She made a disappointed sound.

"Hey, listen. Congratulations. I couldn't be happier for both of you. Mostly for Tony, because he scored an incredible woman who's willing to put up with his crap."

"Aw, thank you. You'll come to the wedding, right? We're not having the whole formal deal, or you'd definitely be in it. It'll just be a casual, no-shoes beach thing. But you're still the best man in spirit. Always."

"I wouldn't miss it for the world."

"What about you, sweetie?" Kelli asked. "Have you found that special someone yet?"

An image of Cagney burst into his mind. He shoved it away. "I'm not looking, Kel," he said, evasively. "I'm a die-hard workaholic. You know that."

"That's nuts. You can't work your life away. What about love? Family? Babies? What about holding a familiar hand in your old age?"

Jonas closed his eyes, trying not to think about the future. He struggled to keep his tone light. "Well, that jerk Tony took the best woman in the world off the market, so what's the point?"

Her effervescent laughter came across the line. "You men. Such players." She paused, and when she spoke again, insightful empathy laced her words. "Still hooked on the one that got away after all these years, huh?"

Shock riddled through Jonas. Why were women so damned perceptive? How did they do it? "I don't know what you're talking about," he lied.

"Oh, you don't, do you?" she asked, pointedly, her crap detector in high-frequency mode. "So, where are you?"

Trapped.

He couldn't make something up. He cleared his throat. "Back in Colorado."

"In your high-school town?" she asked knowingly.

He hung his head back against the chair. "I'm adding a wing onto the medical center here, Kel. That's why I'm here."

"Sure it is. Big of you, considering you supposedly despise the place."

"I do."

"Uh-huh. So, have you seen her yet?"

Jonas hesitated.

"I'll take that as a yes. And is she single?"

He sighed, waving the white flag in his mind. No sense trying to evade her, because she wouldn't back down until she got the answers she wanted. Kelli always got what she wanted. "She is single. But that's not the point."

"Then what is the point, sweetie? And I'm talking the point of life?"

"Look, this isn't some kind of chick flick reunion with Cagney. That's not why I'm here. She broke my heart. Shattered it."

"So what? It was a zillion years ago, wasn't it?"

"Uh…" It stunned him how she could minimize the single biggest soul wound of his life.

"Some prom mix-up, right? This Cagney's probably over it, so you need to get over it, too. Do that whole bygones deal."

His head reeled. "Yeah, well *over it* or not, we come from completely different worlds."

"So? This isn't regency England. Worlds are allowed to overlap in the twenty-first century."

"Maybe so, but I'm still not welcome in hers." He shrugged. "It's no good pushing this one, Kel. Too much baggage. I have to be able to sleep at night, you know? Conscience clear, heart in the right place."

"Oh, I understand that, believe me. Hang on." Her words were muffled as she spoke to Tony in the background. "My demanding soon-to-be-husband wants the phone back, but I have one final question for you before I hand it over. And here's the best part—you don't even have to answer."

"My kind of question." He took a large drink from his beer.

"Well, you don't have to answer me. But you do have to face the truth for yourself."

He braced himself. "Okay, shoot."

"Are you sleeping with a clear conscience and a settled heart now? *Without* her in your life?" She let her words hang there. "Million-dollar question, sweetie."

He felt ill.

"Okay, here's Tony again. We love you, Jonas. Don't forget that."

He forced a swallow past the lump in his throat. "I love you guys, too."

Again with the phone jostling.

"Heart-to-heart with my wife-to-be, eh?" Tony asked, finally back on the line.

"Something like that. You know women— they all want life to be one big fairy tale."

"It can be, bro," Tony said, in an unchar-acteristic moment of seriousness. "Long as you find the right princess."

Jonas blew out a breath. He couldn't take the full court press from his best friend, too. Clearly the Caribbean paradise engagement had affected the man's brain. "Listen, Tony, I'm so glad you called, thrilled Kelli said yes, but I have to go."

A pause. "You okay?"

"Absolutely. I just have a dinner meeting with some members of the hospital board," he lied, in a jovial tone. He was way too

good at saying one thing and feeling another, a skill he wasn't proud of. But sometimes full-bore honesty was overrated.

Tony hesitated. "Okay, but I've told you before and I'll tell you again. You work too damned hard for a thirty-year-old multi-millionaire. All work and no play, buddy. You know what they say about that."

Work was his salvation, all he had. That's what his friends, well-meaning as they were, didn't understand. "I know," he said anyway. "After these projects are done, I'll take some time off, visit you in Margaritaville, chill on the beach with a Corona. Promise."

A moment of companionable silence passed between them.

"Call anytime, man," Tony said. "I mean that. And if you actually need to talk about anything deep or meaningful, I'll put Kelli on."

Jonas laughed. "I will. Let me know as soon as the wedding plans are set so I can block the dates out in my calendar."

They said their goodbyes and hung up.

The sun had dipped behind the now purple peaks during the phone call, leaving bloodred streaks in the sky. He wouldn't have thought it possible, but he felt more

alone right now than he had before the call. Empty. Hollow. Because the truth was, he wasn't sleeping with a clear conscience or a settled heart, and he hadn't been since the moment he'd seen Cagney's face in that parking garage.

It was time for him to do something about it.

His life had never been a fairy tale…but he hadn't reached The End yet.

Time to make things right.

After the horrific workday that ended with her crying silently and Jonas leaving without so much as a goodbye, Cagney officially gave up on the notion of a reconciliation. The effort itself had turned her into someone she didn't want to be, and though making a mental and emotional break from Jonas crushed her heart, she wasn't a stupid woman. She knew a lost cause when she saw one, and she wouldn't continue throwing herself at a man who'd obviously moved on.

So be it. She could move on, too.

Somehow.

She arose extra early the next morning so that Jonas would walk in on her working and not vice versa. She wanted the advantage of being able to say, "Good morning. I'm glad you're here. There's something we need to discuss before we get the day under way."

She hadn't slept much, instead going over exactly what she'd tell him. She had to practice leaching her words of emotion until she came off sounding cool, collected and strong. It had taken hours.

And so it was that Jonas found her already hard at work on the acid-green stripe that next morning. The door opened, and she turned to find him holding a tray of coffee and another bakery bag. He even smiled, albeit tentatively. "Hey."

The thoughtfulness of a cup of coffee and a biscotti or something wasn't going to throw her off her path. She steeled herself for the task ahead. "Hey," she said. Tough, breezy, businesslike. She set her roller aside. "I'm glad you're here. There's something I want to talk to you about."

A ripple of uncertainty moved over his face. He held up the tray. "I come bearing gifts of caffeine and chocolate."

"Great," she said, still on her game. She indicated the floor where they'd sat the night before. "Let's sit for a minute so I can get this off my chest."

He nodded, heading that way. "Yes, I have a few things to say, too. Ladies first, though."

They settled onto the floor, and she thanked him for the coffee and chocolate croissant. Frankly, in such proximity to the love of her life, her nerves set in. She gripped the take-out coffee with all ten spread fingers. It was good to have something to hold on to, to steady herself with. All the better to get through the half lies she was about to tell. She took a sip.

"So, what's up?" Jonas prompted.

She took a deep breath. "Yesterday sucked," she said plainly. "And after you left, I did a lot of soul searching about it."

"So did I," Jonas said.

She shook her head. "Wait. Let me get it all out. Please."

He acquiesced by inclining his head.

"I had it in my mind that you and I would one day find each other again, and we'd talk, reconnect, get beyond all our traumas from the past and realize we'd been perfect for each other all along. Soul mates for all time."

He watched her over the brim of his coffee, nothing but attentiveness and interest in his expression.

"I was wrong," Cagney said. "And I'm sorry."

His face changed.

Cagney wouldn't be able to describe it if asked, but an instantaneous metamorphosis had occurred, for sure. She tried to ignore it, clearing her throat and forging ahead. "It wasn't fair for me to push my ridiculous fantasy on you when the reality is, we've both moved on." She lifted a shoulder. "What could we expect, right? Twelve years. Different life paths and all."

"Right," he answered slowly.

She nodded once to hide the stab of pain. "Good. You agree. And I don't want to drag this out. But I want you to know that I no longer see us as a couple, and it's not something I'm going to push for." She laughed then, nervously. "It was absurd to begin with. We might have started here in the Gulch together, and I won't deny that you were my first love, something I'll always treasure. But years have passed. We belong to vastly different worlds now. You're a successful, jet-setting philanthropist and I'm the quintessential small-town girl. You hate it here, and I'm not going anywhere. You're wealthy, I'm not." She shrugged, as if it were nothing. "It was more than obvious yesterday that you don't think we're a good fit anymore, and, hey, you're probably right. So be it." She twisted her mouth to the side. "I guess I don't need to go on."

"Nope," he said, his demeanor hardened and remote. "All clear on my end."

"Good. Because I want you to know I'm not going to pry into your personal life anymore, and I don't expect anything from you. We're in business together, for the time being anyway." At the quizzical turn to his head, she added, "I mean, once the teen center and art therapy wing are completed, you're leaving Troublesome Gulch, right? On to another philanthropic cause, I assume?"

He hesitated. "Uh, sure. That was the plan from the beginning, yes."

"I want us to be clear with each other from here on out. I'm okay with you leaving. I was acting like a lovesick teenager, banking on an emotional connection that has long since disappeared." A beat passed. "That won't happen again."

"Good. Fine."

"It never would've worked between us anyway, right?"

Jonas shrugged. "That's the word on the street."

A sweeping sadness made Cagney drop her gaze to the top of her coffee mug for several long moments. This felt like an ending she had never wanted to face. A death, really.

"So—" Jonas cleared his throat. "How's this thing going to work between us now? Since you seem to have planned it all out in your head."

She ran her fingers around the white plastic top on her cup, then forced herself to look up. "Just like you wanted. We come in, work together as colleagues. I don't probe into your personal life, and you don't probe into mine. Whatever happened prior to this moment, we let go. At the end of each workday, we each go home and lead our separate lives, just as we've been doing for the past twelve years."

"And that's what you want?" Jonas asked, his tone slightly husky. "That's enough for you?"

No! No! her heart screamed. *I want you, today, tomorrow, for the rest of my life.* "Yes," she said instead, proud of how steady she sounded, of the fact that she didn't crumble. "That's exactly what I want."

"Okay, then. Done."

Just that easy. Cagney took a swallow of coffee, unsure if she could choke it down past the lump in her throat. "Good. Great. Your turn."

"Excuse me?"

"You said you had something to say, too."

"Oh." Jonas looked past her, focusing on nothing, it seemed. "Never mind. It was nothing."

A beat passed. "You're sure?"

"I've never been more sure."

She inhaled strength and exhaled profound sadness. "So, shall we get to work?"

"Absolutely." He stood. "The sooner we get this place finished, the better." He started to walk away.

"Jonas…"

He turned back toward her, slowly.

Nervous, suddenly, she wound her fingers together. "I'm sorry it took me so long to catch on to what you needed from this. And I'm sorry about yesterday."

She watched his Adam's apple rise and fall. "I'm sorry about that, too. Believe me."

She convinced herself that she and Jonas had settled into a workable kind of silence, though really they just started ignoring each other. He seemed to take her talk to heart, which she supposed was a good thing.

He didn't speak to her more than necessary.

She didn't speak to him more than necessary.

They got the job done and stayed out of each other's way. She caught him watching her thoughtfully a few times, and once it seemed as if he might want to talk, but he cut himself off, which was fine with her. No way was she going to wind up right back where they started again.

It was better this way.

Easier.

She'd rather not feel anything than suffer the pain, again, of knowing Jonas didn't want her. God knew, she was the expert of numbing her emotions. The center kept rolling along, that's what mattered.

Faith came through with the tagging crew, just like Faith *always* came through with everything. Her and Brody's foster son, Jason Cole, had agreed to head up the group, and as it happened, their workday fell on the Saturday of her regular monthly dinner party. She was looking forward to the evening, trying out a new recipe—grilled elk steaks—on the usual suspects. Had it been last month, she might have tried to lure, cajole or pressure Jonas into joining them. He'd have declined, and then she would've harassed him about it until they erupted into an argument.

No more.

His nights were his own to spend however he liked. But first, they needed to get the graffiti wall finished and move in some furniture.

Jason had done a rough sketch of the wall, and he brought it to Cagney shyly. "Officer Bishop—"

"Please, call me Cagney." She smiled. "Here at the Teen Center, I'm just Cagney."

The young man licked his lips. "Okay. I wanted to show you and, um, Jonas my idea before the guys get started. Just to make sure…you know." He thrust the paper toward her, head down, clearly worried about her opinion.

He had no reason to be. The drawing was amazing, featuring a kind of futuristic Denver skyline replete with teenage super-heroes, movement and a sense of light and hope. "Jase, this is unbelievable."

His gaze shot toward her face. "I can change it if—"

"No, hon." She rested her palm on his shoulder. "I meant unbelievably *great.*"

An instant look of shock was replaced with pleased astonishment. "No lie? I was worried it would totally suck, since you're a real artist and all."

A stab of lost opportunities nearly bent Cagney over, but she staved it off. "Me? You're the real artist here." She shook her head in wonder. "Do Faith and Brody know how talented you are?"

Jason blushed plum rose. "I just do it for fun."

"Well, you should think about doing it for a living. Truly. This is staggering." She eyed him. "You have college to think about next year, yes?"

He nodded.

"Tell Faith I said you should apply to the Art Institute of Colorado. You're too good not to. Actually, I'll tell her myself when I see her tonight."

He blew out a big sigh. "Cool, man. Thanks." He eyed his sketch, then peered up at her uncertainly. "You really think I could do something like this for a living?"

"With some training? Absolutely. On another day, you and I can talk about all the job opportunities open to artists."

"Cool." They shared another smile. "Um, can we get Jonas to sign off on the sketch, too?" Jase asked, aiming his thumb over his shoulder at the man, "so the guys can start sketching it in?"

She felt her smile fade, but couldn't stop it from happening. She flashed a glance toward the enigmatic Jonas, embroiled in setting up the computer section, remote as ever. "Ah, sure. Why don't you take it over and show it to him. I'm going to hit that furniture truck outside and get some stuff moved in. Divide and conquer, know what I mean?"

"Uh, sure. Okay. But   "

"What is it?"

Jason peered uncertainly from her to Jonas and back. "Do you think he'll dig it, too? I mean, maybe you should say something. Weigh in, you know?"

She huffed, then gave Jase's shoulder a squeeze. "Trust me, I have no idea what the man likes, kiddo, so whatever I'd say wouldn't matter. But regardless of what he thinks, that masterpiece is going on the wall. Okay?"

Jason's gaze darted around. "Okay. Even if he hates it?"

"Even then. But he won't hate it." She touched his back. "Go on."

The boy ambled away. Cagney pushed Jonas out of her head and hustled outside. She needed to throw herself into something mind-numbing. Heart-numbing. Soul-numbing.

Several hours later, all the Foofs had been moved in and arranged, as had the game table, the homework carrels, the dinette set. The television and stereo system had been installed and tested, and she was at the tail end of soundchecking the karaoke machine and stage lights.

All without exchanging a single word with Jonas.

It should've felt like a triumph, but it didn't.

It just felt lonely.

Miraculously, the five taggers—Jason Cole included—had completed the graffiti wall in record time. It looked beautiful, better than she'd even expected after having seen the sketch. The boys had added shading and light, detail that made the art jump off the wall. She thanked them profusely, handing them each an envelope of cash for their considerable services. She invited them to hang out, even offered to get ice cream, but one after the other, the boys mumbled their weak excuses, then bolted.

Kids. Never wanted to hang around and just chat.

Maybe it was the cop thing.

A while later, Cagney pushed her fists into her aching lower back to stretch it. She *had* to speak to Jonas now, unfortunately. After so many days of nothing, the simplest conversation felt foreign on her tongue. Uncomfortable. "Can you lock up? I have plans tonight and I need to head upstairs and get ready."

He didn't even lift his head from the computer station he'd been working on. "Whatever you need."

She didn't move, instead resting one foot atop the other. "The kids did a great job, don't you think?"

"Yup."

Nice show of enthusiasm. "Do you like the layout of all the furniture?"

He didn't even look. "However you arrange it is fine."

"Okay. Well…see ya."

He merely grunted

Cagney told herself she couldn't care less. It was what she'd asked for. She took the freight elevator up to her sanctuary determined to put the tension of the day behind her and prepare for a fabulous dinner party with people who loved her for who she was. Jonas wasn't her problem anymore.

So why did this hurt so much?

She'd scrubbed the loft until it shone the night before, so she poured a much-needed glass of wine, ran a bath, and set her sights directly forward. Fun, friends, food.

Her new positive plan for a happy life.

Who needed love anyway, right?

Jonas sat in his car outside Cagney's loft in the dark and watched her through the floor-to-ceiling windows on the second level. Freshly showered and wearing something black and flowy, she bustled through the place lighting candles, arranging flowers, opening bottles of wine to breathe. Did she know just how visible her life was from the street? Did she care?

God, she was beautiful.

Headlights flashed in his rearview mirror. He swore and hunkered down just as Lexy arrived in her van, parking directly behind him, of course. Once she was safely inside the loft, he drove away blacked out. The others would be showing up soon, and he had no desire to get busted staring up at Cagney like some Peeping Tom freak.

But seeing her up there, moving around her beautiful home, he'd never wanted anything as much as he wanted inclusion in Cagney's world right then. Instead, he was on the outside looking in.

Typical.

She had a circle of friends, a life, a sanctuary.

He had an empty hotel suite. Empty, save all the regrets crowded into the dark corners like piles of dirty laundry.

Unfortunately, things had gone so awry between them, he didn't know how to begin to fix it. Cagney had made it painfully obvious she was over him, and he'd decided the least he could do for her was respect that. For himself, too. Her little chat had felt like a repeat of the letter she'd left for him on prom night. Civil, polite, but straight to the bone. He couldn't handle it a third time.

So, instead of sucking up his pride and telling Cagney he'd had a change of heart that day and he'd like to start over, he'd agreed to her terms without argument.

Path of least resistance.

Way to go, Jonas.

It should've cleared up so many problems in his life, but instead it seemed to compound them. And he didn't see a damn way around it.

Sad and knowing his work with the youth center was coming to an end, he drove slowly back to Crested Butte. Alone.

After everyone had arrived and had wineglasses in hand, Nate and Brody gravitated toward the living room and the women toward the kitchen. Par for the course, but Cagney loved the ritual of it. The loft bustled with energy and conversation and laughter, the kitchen redolent with delicious scents.

This was what life was about.

She didn't have to feel the least bit melancholy about being alone, because she wasn't. Not really.

Who are you trying to convince?

She gulped against the thought.

"Need any help?" Lexy asked, maneuvering her chair toward the prep island in the wide-open kitchen. Faith and Erin followed, each carrying their babies.

"No, thanks. I just have to toss the salad. The elk steaks should be done any time now." She flashed what she hoped was a festive smile at her friends. "But I appreciate the company. What's new with you all?"

"Nothing on my end." A pause. "The teen center looks amazing so far," Erin said, switching gears.

"Yeah, it's really coming along," Cagney said, striving for cheer. It sounded false to her, though. She'd really rather not talk about the center or anything having to do with, well, the pathetic state of her life, truth be told.

In her peripheral vision, she caught a glance exchanged between Erin and Faith. Cagney's gaze darted from one to the other, suddenly wary. "What?"

"What, what?" Faith replied, blinking innocently.

"The look." She pointed her finger between the two of them. "You guys exchanged a look. And don't try to deny it. I've known you way too long."

For a moment, no one said anything.

"Just tell me." She nailed Erin with a stare. "It's the teen center, right? Do you hate the bright colors? Is the furniture wrong?"

Faith cleared her throat. Erin flicked a glance her way, then handed baby Nate to Lexy. "No, everything really looks great, scout's honor."

Cagney studied her friends, trying to read between the lines. When she couldn't, she went back to her salad tongs. "Okay, but you exchanged a look. I know you did."

"How's the actual work process coming along?" Erin asked cryptically.

Cagney's hands stilled over the salad. She looked to Lexy and Faith, but neither would meet her gaze. "It's fine. Busy. Why do you ask?"

Erin crossed her arms. "Just making conversation."

She uttered a sound of frustration. "Yes, but what did you *mean?* You guys just told me the place looks great. Stop beating around the bush."

"She meant the working relationship," Lexy explained, gently. "Between you and Jonas."

"Oh." Cagney tensed immediately. "Jonas is Jonas. We're…the same as always. All business. I don't really want to talk about him, if you don't mind."

"The thing is," Faith interjected, "you two are running that place. Together."

"For now." She shrugged. "He's leaving Troublesome Gulch as soon as both projects are done."

"Really?" Lexy asked. "That seems odd, because I saw him speaking to Miranda Welks the other day at lunchtime."

Cagney's stomach dropped. She schooled her features as best she could. "Well, maybe they're dating."

"Why would Jonas date Miranda Welks?" Faith asked.

"Didn't look like a date," Lexy continued, passing over Faith's question. "He was sitting inside her real-estate office across the desk from her, and she was printing things off and handing them over. Showing him listings, I'd assume."

"Besides, if they were dating, wouldn't you know?" Erin interjected.

"No," Cagney said softly. "We don't talk about stuff like that. It's none of my business what he does in his spare time. What's this all about anyway?"

Faith cleared her throat. "Brody and I spoke with Jason today after he came home from the little graffiti session, asked him how it went and so on."

Her chest tightened. "He's an amazing

artist. All the boys did a great job." No comments from her pals. Suddenly, Cagney felt the prickle of defensiveness along her spine. "What did Jason say?"

Faith scrunched her nose apologetically. "He said the painting part was cool, but that he and the other boys couldn't wait to 'jet.'"

Cagney blinked. "Jet?"

"Leave," Faith explained. "As in, leave the center. I'm sorry to have to tell you."

Cagney's hands started to shake. She set the salad tongs aside, her mind completely off the food, then took a large gulp of her wine. Her legs felt weak, so she leaned against the refrigerator. This came as a huge blow. She'd so banked on the teen center being a huge success, on maybe being a whole new career for her. The thought of returning to patrol duty made her want to cry. "So, our first test teens don't like the center? That's just swell. Did he happen to mention why they don't like it?"

"Oh, no." Faith held up one hand. "They think the place rocks. It's just…"

"They didn't feel comfortable there," Erin blurted.

Shock radiated through Cagney. "What? How could they not? I did everything to make them feel at home." She glanced around at each of her friends in turn. There'd been no arguments between the boys. No snipping of any sort. She hadn't hovered at all. On the contrary, she'd let them do their thing and had even brought in lunch and offered to buy ice cream. Her eyes narrowed as she studied the group of women she knew and loved. "Wait a minute. You guys discussed this whole thing already, didn't you? Behind my back."

They all nodded. Sheepishly.

"God, it feels like an intervention." Her self-protectiveness kicked up a notch. "Well, then, spit it out. I've busted my butt to create a fun, safe haven, and if it's not working, I want to know why." She looked pointedly from friend to friend. "What's wrong with the center?"

"It's you and Jonas," Erin said, reluctantly.

That, she hadn't expected. It took three blinks and another swallow of wine before she could ask, "Excuse me?"

"Jason said the tension level between you two reminded him of being home with his parents, and you know how horrific his home life was." Faith tilted her head sympathetically. "I'm so sorry. That's exactly what the boy said."

Mortified by her friend's words, Cagney nevertheless flicked her hand. Obviously this was something she needed to hear, painful or not. Something that needed to be corrected. "Stop apologizing. Just tell me everything he said."

Faith reached out and held her hand. "The thing is, Cag, these kids come from homes rife with stress and tension and all that crammed-down, unsaid stuff—"

"I know they do," she said sharply. Too sharply. She took a deep breath and lightened her tone. "Believe me, if anyone understands that, I do. Jonas and I don't fight."

"You don't speak to each other, either, apparently."

They all watched Cagney in silence.

"You know what I'm talking about," Faith said.

Cagney's heart fluttered up near her throat. She thought they'd been so careful, cheerful and civil enough. But adults always thought that, didn't they? *The kids can't hear us, they think everything's just fine.* "Of course I do, but—"

"The kids who are going to use the center are especially attuned to that kind of subtext," Lexy said.

"Yes," Cagney murmured.

"Well, apparently the acrimony was radiating off of you and Jonas big-time. Like gasoline off hot pavement."

"That's not going to work if you want the center to be a respite for those kids," Erin added, though she didn't need to say anything.

"There wasn't really any acrimony," Cagney said in a weak tone. "Jonas and I have just worked out…a way of dealing with each other."

"By pretending the other person doesn't exist?" Faith asked.

Cagney dropped her gaze to the hardwood floor. "I wouldn't go that far," she murmured, knowing it was a lie.

Faith twisted her lips to the side. "Well, those were Jason's words, not mine."

Hearing this from her friends hurt— Cagney couldn't deny it. She felt like a failure. But when she'd left her parents' home, she'd vowed she wouldn't perpetuate their lifestyle, no matter what. She sucked in one side of her cheek, remembering how she could assess the tone of the evening just from her father's body language. Still could.

God, she and Jonas were falling into the same trap.

How in the hell had that happened?

She thought they'd hammered everything out.

She blew out a breath and crossed her ankles, then hung her head.

"Don't be upset," Faith pleaded.

"I'm not. Well, I am. But mostly I'm disgusted. With myself, with Jonas, with the fact that we both grew up in those kinds of dysfunctional environments, and yet we're too damn clueless to notice when we're laying the exact same trip on those poor kids."

"I'm sorry we had to be the ones to tell you," Erin said.

Cagney lifted her chin and braved a smile, though she really needed to be alone and process this. "No. Don't be. Seriously. It was just the wake-up slap I needed. As much as we've vowed to be all business, it seems Jonas and I are letting our personal issues poison the place before it even opens. That's wrong."

"I'm sure it was just a bad day," Faith, the eternal optimist, said.

"I wish that were true, but it has turned into a bad situation all the way around. Today was just like every other day, I hate to say."

She braved her way through her friends'

clucking sympathy. "Not to worry, though. I'm going to fix it, whatever it takes. Even if it means bowing out of the project altogether."

"You can't do that!" Erin said.

"I'm committed to the center. I'll do whatever it takes to make it a success. Even that. Anyway, thank you." Cagney bent down to Lexy's level in her wheelchair and opened her arms for a group hug. The other women followed suit. "I love you guys and I want to do this thing right. I appreciate you having my back."

The four embraced, awkwardly around the babies.

"Always," Erin said, with a meaningful glance after they'd broken apart. "And I mean that. You've done so much for me and Nate and the baby, it's the least we can do."

Cagney laughed, but the sound lacked the requisite humor. "Tough love, huh?"

One side of Erin's mouth lifted. "Something like that."

"I'll take care of it. Promise." She touched Faith's arm, smiling tremulously. "Tell Jase how sorry I am. God, I'd been patting myself on the back for doing such a good job. Now I feel like my father's little clone."

"Please. You're nothing like Chief."

Cagney fought back the lump in her throat. "Well, it turns out I'm more my father's daughter than I ever thought I would be." She inhaled deeply. "Anything else you need to tell me before we eat?"

"One thing," Erin said, in a grave tone.

Cagney braced herself.

"Those Foofs are freakin' awesome."

The four women laughed out loud, breaking enough of the tension that they could move on.

"I know they are. That's why we bought them." She clapped her hands together once, determined to enjoy the rest of the evening, no matter how improbable "enjoyment" seemed at this point. "Now, enough shop talk. I need downtime badly." Cagney craned her neck around her friends and smiled at Brody and Nate, who were embroiled in some sort of guy debate that required them to sit on the edges of their seats and gesture broadly. "Hey, guys," she called out. "Dinner's served."

Everyone moved en masse toward the festively set table while Cagney took the steaks off the broiler. For the first time in the history of her monthly dinner parties, she couldn't wait for this evening to end.

She had plans to coordinate. Big ones.

Chapter Eight

Jonas's cell phone rang just after one in the morning. He would have liked to say it awakened him from a deep, restful sleep, but no. He'd been lying in bed in his dark hotel suite, watching crappy late-night reruns and wondering what Cagney and her friends were doing, how much fun they were having. Pathetic with a capital *P*. He flipped open the phone without checking caller ID. "Jonas here."

"We need to talk," she said without preamble.

He propped himself up straighter on one elbow. "Cagney?"

"Yeah, it's me." She sighed. "Sorry to bother you. Can you come back to the Gulch?"

He ran his fingers through his hair and shot a glance at the digital alarm clock on the nightstand. "Now? Do you know what time it is?"

"Jonas, it's important or I wouldn't have called, I promise. I can drive there if you'd prefer, but I had two glasses of wine before dinner, and I don't usually—"

"No, I wouldn't want that. I'll drive there." He stood, already scoping out the blue-shadowed room to locate his earlier discarded jeans. "Is everything okay?"

"Nothing's okay." She sounded exhausted. "But I don't want to talk about it over the phone."

"Okay. I'll be there in half an hour or so." He paused, jolting upright. "We didn't have a break-in, did we?"

"Nothing like that. I'll tell you everything when you get here. Just hurry, okay?"

Thirty-eight minutes later, he walked into the teen center and found Cagney sitting cross-legged on the bright orange Foof, her hands wrapped around a mug of coffee. She wore green cotton pajama pants with little brown monkeys on them and a brown tank top that left little to the imagination, not that he was complaining. Her thick, blond hair tumbled loose over her shoulders.

She glanced up when he entered the space, her expression pensive. She tried for a smile, but fell short. "Hey."

"Hey."

She lifted her chin toward a thermal carafe sitting on the counter of the kitchenette. "There's fresh coffee if you want some. Baileys right next to it."

He walked over to the counter and poured himself a cup, just for something to do. He added a solid slug of the liqueur, figuring he might need it. Her funereal demeanor amped his stress level, yet he found himself stalling rather than pressing her for the reasons why she was so down. Clearly something awful had happened for Cagney to have called him in the middle of the night, and he'd had enough of awful, especially with her.

After settling onto the plum-colored Foof across from her, he blew the steam from his mug, then took a sip of the laced brew. "How was your dinner party?"

She peered at him curiously. "Enlightening. How'd you know I was having a dinner party?"

"I have ears, and they work. How was it enlightening?"

She twisted her mouth to the side. "Well, that's why I called, actually. We have a big problem."

"We, meaning you and me?"

She nodded. "The center, really. But yeah, you and me, bottom line."

He cocked his head. "A permit thing? Something with Chief?"

"Nope. Far worse than either of those. A client thing."

"Meaning?"

Her shoulders raised on a breath, then dropped. "The kids hate the place."

Shock zinged through him. "What kids? The boys today?"

She nodded slowly.

Impossible. "What could they possibly hate about it?"

"Us."

"Us?"

"You're repeating me, just so you know, but yes." After shoring up her resolve, she told him everything her friends had said in all its ugly detail.

By the end of it, he felt as devastated as she looked. He knew neither of them had ever wanted to perpetuate the cycle of family dysfunction, and yet they hadn't managed to catch themselves falling into its trap. How had that happened?

He swore, then ran a palm down his face. "This sucks."

"To put it mildly."

"We have to turn it around."

"I agree."

He gulped. "What are we going to do?"

"Well, I've thought about that all evening." She set her coffee mug on a side table and tucked her hair behind both ears. "I think we have a couple of choices. First option, I can back out of the project. Let Chief assign another cop to work the place since he's so gung-ho on a police presence, which frankly I don't agree with." She slashed her hands out to the side. "Whole different issue. Anyway, I can quit, another cop takes over, and I'll go back to patrol."

"No way. You love this assignment. It wouldn't be the same without you. Besides, you made a strong case for why this needed to be your project. Backing off now would give Chief too much satisfaction." A pause.

"I'll leave." It killed him to say it. He didn't want to abandon the project. More importantly, he couldn't imagine not seeing Cagney every day and, the way things had been going, this was the only way he'd be able to. They might not be on the best of terms at the moment, but seeing her daily was still the high point in his pathetic, lonely life.

"That won't work, either." She twisted her mouth to one side. "I can't fund the place without you, Jonas, to be frank and crass about it. Besides, it was your baby first. I just jumped on the bandwagon."

"It's your house," he countered. "And I'll still foot the bills."

"Not fair. It was your idea." She made an expression of distaste. "I wouldn't feel right about that financial arrangement anyway."

He held up a palm. "Okay, stalemate. Neither of us wants to leave. Do I have that straight?"

She sighed. "Yes."

"So, what other choices do we have?"

She gave him a sad smile. "There's only one I can think of, and I'm sure you're not going to like it."

"Try me."

She bit her lip, studying him for several long, excruciating moments. "For both of us to remain involved with the center and really make it work, we need to repair our relationship. For real this time. Clear the air, once and for all. We need to be friends again—true friends, Jonas, like we used to be. And if we can't get to that place, then we'll never be able to run the teen center like it should be run, so we'll have to abandon the project altogether. Because I can't stand for anything less with it. It's too important to me."

Jonas considered this. She was right. Completely. And the interesting thing was he felt grateful for the opportunity to rectify things.

"Okay, I'll start with the reparations."

Her shoulders dropped with relief. "Really? That easily?"

"Yes." He blew out a long breath. "I'm truly sorry for how I acted the day your father showed up here. I don't know what got into me. I guess I'm a little—"

"Defensive?"

He gave her a pained look. "Yeah," he said through clenched teeth.

She nodded. "Apology accepted. I've been known to dip my toes into the defensiveness pool myself. And I'm sorry I've been giving you the cold shoulder ever since. I just… didn't know how to deal."

"It's okay."

"No, see, it isn't," she said vehemently. "We need to set higher standards for ourselves if this is going to work." She leaned in, adamant. "I guess I should ask you before we go any further. Do you want to work through this? Do you honestly want our friendship back?"

He studied the play of light on the soft curves of her face. "I do, Cag. I really do."

Her cheeks warmed to a rosy hue. "Good. The thing is, I wasn't completely forthright with you when I cut things off. I implied I was over you, but that was my own self-protection talking. I want our friendship back, too, Jonas," she said beseechingly. "I have missed you so much—" she pressed her lips together, then shook her head. "There aren't even words to express how much. But it can't be halfway. We can't keep this impenetrable wall between us. I need a few honest answers from you if our friendship is ever going to heal."

Ignoring the warning thud in his chest, he inclined his head. "Ask away, then. I'll do my best to answer."

She leveled him with a sad stare. "Why didn't you visit me in the hospital after the prom night crash?"

Kick to the gut, that question. He whistled low through his teeth. "That far back, huh?"

"Might as well start at the beginning. The beginning of the end, that is."

He gulped back his dread about reopening these long-festering wounds. Had to be examined, cleaned and sutured back up, he supposed. "The truth? I didn't even know there had been a crash until several years after the fact."

Her eyes widened. "Years? How can that be?"

Here it was. The ugly moment of truth. "After I came to pick you up for prom and had it out with your father—"

"Wait. What did he say to you?" Her eyes narrowed to slits.

"Let me answer one question at a time. Please."

She inclined her head.

He regrouped. "Anyway, after that fiasco, I went straight home and packed up Mom and our stuff. We left that night."

She gaped, looking astonished. "Just drove off?"

He nodded.

"I can't even…comprehend that."

"We didn't own much, as you know. It was an impulsive reaction by a crushed teenage boy. I know that now. But at the time, all I wanted was to be as far away from Troublesome Gulch as possible. Mom didn't care. She never did have much of her own will. I figured she and I would find our way to wherever as we drove."

"And you ended up in Seattle? Just like magic?"

"Well, sort of. The next morning, Mom woke up—I was driving, of course—and we discussed our unplanned plans. She said she'd always liked the idea of Puget Sound." He lifted one shoulder. "I didn't know the first thing about it, but it seemed as logical a reason as any to choose a new place to live. So we headed northwest. We actually lived on Bainbridge Island because it was less expensive."

She blinked, seeming to struggle with wrapping her brain around the whole thing. "And told no one?"

"I'd cut ties with everyone in the Gulch. Well, tie—singular. I mean, you were my only true connection."

Spots of red blotched her cheeks.

"And Mom didn't have any friends here." He paused to watch Cagney whisk away a tear. His stomach cramped. "Please don't cry. It kills me when you cry. It's one of the few things that makes a guy feel so god-awful helpless."

"I don't mean to. I just feel sorry for Ava."

He pushed back a wave of his own emotion. "Yeah. Well." He paused. "That's why I never heard anything about the crash. Several years later, the Seattle paper ran some sort of exposé about prom night fatalities nationwide. They highlighted yours since so many kids…died."

"Troublesome Gulch made the Seattle paper. Wow."

"Pretty major accident. I mean, look how it changed things here. A paid fire department, paid paramedic battalion. Level Two trauma center." He flipped his hand over. "Never had that stuff back in the day."

"Yeah." She twisted her lips to the side. "Too bad those services weren't in place to save my friends. It always takes a tragedy to wake people the hell up."

He squeezed his eyes shut before leaning forward imploringly. "God, I couldn't even breathe, Cag, until I'd read all the way through the article and learned that you hadn't been one of the fatalities. I was sick about it. If I'd known about the accident when it happened, screw your father. I'd have been there. You have to believe me."

"I do, and it clears up some of the pain in my heart."

"Too little, too late?"

She gave a small, sad smile. "No. Thank you for telling me that." A quizzical far-off look came over her face.

"What are you thinking?"

"I guess I still don't understand why you left that night, so spur of the moment. Why you didn't stay at least until we had a chance to talk?"

"I left you messages all that day," he said. "You never replied, and you didn't show up at school."

"Yeah, because I was under house arrest," she said, her words laced with frustration. "Chief had taken away all means of communication. My cell phone, the home phone. The computer. I wasn't even allowed out of my room. You knew how he operated. I guess I just thought you would've figured out that something was up. I would never blow off your calls unless I had no way to return them. I thought you knew that."

Jonas's head started to swirl. "Why were you under house arrest?"

She spread her arms wide. "Because he found out you and I were going to prom together from one of his stupid spies, probably, and he was livid."

Jonas's turn to feel confused. "B-but, you went with Tad. I know you did."

"Yes." Cagney untucked her legs from beneath her and moved over to sit tentatively on the edge of his Foof. "Jonas, Chief forced me to go with another date or not at all," she said, softly. "I tried to go stag with my friends so I could—"

"Why didn't you skip it?"

"Just listen. Please." She pleaded with her eyes. "I didn't stay home because that's what he wanted, for me to sit alone and wallow. I was stubborn. Maybe even stupid. But my plan was to call you once I escaped the house, explain everything, and we could hook up at the dance…presumptuous, I know. And really unfair and unkind to Tad, but I wasn't thinking about him. I was only thinking about you. Us."

He looked down, glum.

"Jonas—" she gulped "—I would've told Chief to go to hell about the whole thing, but he threatened me."

His narrowed gaze shot to her face.

She nodded. "He said if I went to prom with you, he wouldn't pay for my college. Not a dime. I wouldn't have been able to go to CSU at all."

Shock radiated through him. "Are you kidding me?"

"I wish. He knew the only thing that would keep me from going to prom with you was dangling my freedom over my head." She paused. "Which I would've explained to you if only you'd called me back. I didn't have a chance to call you until after everyone picked me up, of course, and then I didn't have my own cell phone, so—"

"You borrowed Tad's," he said, in a distant tone.

"Yes. And the whole thing was so unfair to Tad. I made the poor kid feel like an also-ran on the last night of his life." She pounded a fist against her thigh. "I *still* feel horrible about that." She reached out and took one of his hands, pressing it between her own. "Please talk to me. Tell me what's going through your head."

"That I wish I'd called you back. Then again, I can't say I regret how most of my life played out, except for things between you and me. I don't know. It's all a jumble."

"At the time, I figured you'd rather have our whole college lives together than one stupid dance—"

"I would have," he said, his tone husky.

"But I never got the chance to explain that to you—"

"Because I never called. I get it."

"And then you left," she said softly, "the crash happened and my life just—" she shrugged "—imploded. Everything changed once I got out of the hospital, but I never, ever stopped wanting to be with you."

A horrible sort of silence stretched between them like clotheslines draped with the tattered, faded garments of regret and missed opportunities.

Elements remained that still made no sense, though. Namely, the letter.

Oh, no.

No.

He searched her face, as everything started clicking horribly into place. Part of him didn't want to find out if his whole life had been based on lies, but he had to know, once and for all. Had to ask. No matter how much the truth scared him.

"Cagney, if you loved me," he asked cautiously, "then why did you leave that letter?"

She blinked, startled. Total confusion showed in her gaze, and his stomach sank. He knew.

"Letter?"

His breathing shallowed. He saw stars. God, he'd been duped in the worst way. "The letter to me, about how you'd fallen for Tad," he said urgently, almost wanting her to suddenly remember it. He watched her start to shake her head slowly, her eyes widening, but forged ahead despite the loud buzz sounding in his ears. "Torn from your notebook with purple lines that smelled like grapes? The letter you left for me on prom night."

"Jonas, I never wrote you a letter."

"I read it—"

"No. You have to be mistaken. I didn't love Tad. He was a nice kid, but he meant nothing to me. And he died because of it. I'll always feel sad about that, but *you* were my boyfriend. Not Tad. Not ever."

"God, Cag." He hung his head.

Her grip on his hand tightened. "You have to be remembering incorrectly about this letter. Please tell me it's some sort of a misunderstanding."

He looked up, resignation on his face, then pulled his hand from hers. He extracted his wallet from his back pocket.

Cagney sucked in a breath and covered her mouth with both hands.

He eased out that worn sheet of spiral notebook paper, his apparently false talisman throughout the years, unfolded it and handed it to her without another word. "It doesn't smell like grapes anymore, but it's all there."

The paper shook in her hands as she read it, the horror moving over her expression like clouds over a valley. When she reached the end, she dropped the letter and covered her face with both hands, visibly shaking.

"Talk to me," he said.

"I didn't write it, Jonas. I swear on my life."

"Cag, it's in your handwriting."

"Which is identical to my mom's."

"Why would your mom—?"

"He *made* her do it. It's the only explanation. Because I didn't write this."

He squeezed his eyes shut, swathed in loss. Somehow, he'd known she'd say that.

She slid her palms from her face, and now she just looked angry. "He destroyed

lives, and we fell for it. Damn it! We fell for it. I loved you, Jonas, more th anything in this world. I wanted to spend th rest of my life with you, and he stole that from me. From both of us. He stole my art from me. My education. He stole everything."

"Shh, it's okay," Jonas said, not believing his own words. Immobilized with freezing rage, his world tipped on its axis. He reached out and smoothed his hand over her hair. It was all he knew to do. He'd lost the only girl he'd ever truly loved because of a cruel man's incomprehensible manipulations. He needed to focus on consoling Cagney right then, or he just might get into his car, drive to Chief's house and throttle the man. Or worse.

"Jonas, please believe me. About the letter."

"I do. I just…it's been a part of my psyche for so long, I don't know what to do about it."

For a long time, they were both silent, suffocating in their own horrifying realizations and regrets.

"We have to get back at him," Cagney said, a knife-edge of determination in her tone.

"Why bother? He already ruined everything. Besides, revenge is overrated, trust me."

"It's not revenge. It's just showing him that he doesn't control the whole universe. It's about me breaking free."

He considered this. God knew, he had his own taste for breaking free—or whatever Cagney wanted to call it—where Chief was concerned. "What did you have in mind?"

"Well…" She bit one corner of her lip. "Let's pretend he *didn't* ruin everything between us. Make him think all his manipulations failed in the end."

He tilted his head dubiously. "Don't you think it's pretty clear he succeeded?"

"He might think so now," she said thoughtfully as she twirled a lock of her hair around one index finger. "But if we pretend to be back together—"

"Are you crazy?"

She held up a hand. "Just listen. Okay?"

He hesitated, emotions warring inside him. Was he setting himself up for more pain? Then again, what could it hurt to hear her out? He nodded once.

"The Police Ball is next week. Big black-tie affair, dinner, all that. I never go, because *he's* there, holding court and acting like Mr. Wonderful, and it makes me sick."

"I don't blame you."

"Let's go together," she implored him. "You as my date. Pretend date," she hurried to clarify. "But we'll play it for all the world as if it couldn't be more real. It'll be a million times better than the prom since it's his turf, and there's nothing he can do to keep us away. I work for that department, and I can bring whomever I want."

"I don't know, Cag."

"If we want to infuriate the man, that'll do it. Guaranteed. And right now, damn it, I'm yearning for some good, old-fashioned paybacks."

Jonas considered the outlandish idea. So many ways this could decimate his life in the end. Were the so-called paybacks worth it? "It's risky."

"Come on. The only person it can hurt is Chief."

He wasn't sure she'd examined it from all angles.

"It would kill him to think you and I had rekindled our romance after he went to such lengths to destroy it. Tell the truth. Doesn't that sound gratifying?"

He half smiled, but his gut still felt tight. "It does."

"Say you'll do it."

A long, tense pause ensued.

"Okay. Why not?" Screw Chief. He'd do this for himself, just to be with Cagney for one night, all dressed up like they should've been on prom night.

Her whole body relaxed. "Awesome. It'll be great. Just wait. And we can set the groundwork for the so-called reconciliation this week by being seen together all over town."

He nodded. "I think I'll go through with my plans to buy property here, too. Can't have too many real-estate investments. And it's sure to annoy him."

"Ah, so you *were* looking at property," she said.

He cocked his head at her in question.

Her face flamed pink. "Oh. Lexy mentioned she saw you looking at listings in Miranda Welks's office."

He sucked in one side of his cheek. "Wow, that small-town grapevine is alive and well."

She smirked. "You know it. And we can use it to our advantage this week, kill two birds with one stone."

"How so?"

"Once the whole town thinks we're back together, which they will if we play it right, word will spread throughout the teenage community that it's cool to come back to the center because you and I aren't acting like tense, dysfunctional adults. *And* we'll infuriate my father. It's perfect, Jonas. It really is."

They both seemed to hold their breath for a moment.

"You're right," Jonas said finally. "Okay, I'm in. All the way. Whatever it takes."

She released a whoosh of relief and broke into a huge smile. "Thank you. This is going to work. I promise." In her excitement, she leaned in and pressed her lips lightly to his, shocking his body straight to its core. She tasted the same, like home and hope and everything that had ever been good in his life. The taste of her kisses was an imprint on his soul.

As she pulled away, he caught her upper arm and held gently. Their gazes tangled, the fire of attraction licking between them. He saw her breathing go shallow. Color rose to her chest in delicate blotches, a clear indication that she was as turned on as he was. Now wasn't the time to lose control, but he had to taste her again. Had to.

Slowly, never looking away from her eyes, Jonas leaned closer and kissed her, deeper this time, trying to tell her with his mouth everything he couldn't say with words.

She melted into his chest, opening into the kiss. He could feel her nipples harden against him, and it hit him like a sledgehammer: he'd never wanted to make love to someone as much as he did right then.

But that wasn't part of the plan.

He pulled away, shaky with desire and nearly undone from her moan of protest. "Sorry. That was for the prom night kiss I missed." He paused. "But, I should go."

"Don't," she said, her lips moist and swollen. "It's late, I mean."

He flipped his wrist to look at his watch and raised his eyebrows. "Wow, it's later than I thought."

"You can stay in my guest room." She peered up at him through her lashes. "Or—"

"The guest room is fine." He smoothed the backs of his fingers down her cheek. "It wouldn't be smart for us, Cag," he said, knowing he didn't need to explain further. They were on the same page, tied by the same attraction. "A plot to put your father in his place is one thing, but—"

"I understand. Really. I told Faith I'd be satisfied with having your friendship back, and I meant it." She gave him a tremulous smile. "If we're lucky, Chief will drive by in the morning and see your car parked outside, draw his own conclusions. It'll get the whole ball rolling."

He studied the faded letter for a moment, then crushed it in his fist and threw it aside with a flash of anger. "The old bastard deserves whatever pain comes his way. He's hurt a lot of people."

"He can't hurt us anymore, now that we've talked it out." She stood, taking his hand and guiding him up, with her. "Come on. Let's get some sleep. We're going to need our wits about us to lock horns effectively with Chief. He might be a jerk, but he's a smart and calculating one."

He followed her to the freight elevator, not sure he'd ever have his wits fully in order being this close to her, this connected to her.

At the second floor, she pulled the elevator doors opened. "This is my stop." She smiled, sadly. "The guest suite is on the third floor. Can't miss it."

They stared at each other for several long moments, then Jonas backed against the elevator wall, as far from her as he could get. Their attraction to each other had grown exponentially during their time apart, and it was clear they wanted each other with the mature confidence of adults rather than the shy need for exploration of two innocent teens. They'd talked through their wounds of the past and forgiven each other. Everything logically pointed to him stepping off that elevator and joining her in bed, sating both their needs. But he'd done a lot of growing up over the years, and he knew instinctively that they needed a fresh start if things would ever progress from lust to something more. They had to take things slow and get to know each other as the adults they were now, not the kids they used to be.

"'Night, Cag," he whispered, hoping she understood. "Get some rest." He aimed toward the third floor. "I'll see you in the morning."

She exhaled with what he seemed to be the same level of sexual frustration he felt, but she smiled, too. "Okay. Should be all stocked up there. Let me know if you need something, though. Anything," she added, letting the blatant offer trail off as she exited the elevator and closed the doors behind her.

Jonas buried his face in his hands as the

elevator ascended, wondering just what in the heck he'd gotten himself into with this plan of Cagney's. Now he was tasked with *pretending* to love the only woman he'd *ever* loved, all while keeping things "just friends" between them in reality. And that was the last thing he wanted to do.

Seriously, could his life get any more complicated?

Chapter Nine

In an effort to get the rumor mill cranking at full speed, Cagney and Jonas decided to make an early morning appearance at the Pinecone Diner for coffee. They walked there from the loft, enjoying the warmth of the late-summer sunshine and seizing the opportunity to be seen while they strolled. Just before they arrived at the diner, Cagney reached out. "Hold my hand."

Jonas stumbled. "What?"

She smirked. "It's this thing couples do when they're into each other, Jonas. They hold hands."

"Smart aleck." He reached for her hand, yanked her closer, and draped his arm across her shoulders instead, pleased when she blinked up at him in surprise. "It's this thing couples do, Cagney, after they've just spent a torrid night together in bed." He planted a kiss on the top of her head. "Much better gossip generator than a little hand-holding, don't you think?"

"Uh…"

"Slip your hand in my back pocket."

He watched her swallow, then felt her small hand slide into the back pocket of his jeans. "That's the ticket."

Jonas caught a glimpse of the diner's interior from outside before they entered. Packed, as usual. Half of him revved with excitement, the other half prickled with apprehension. But there was no turning back now, and in truth, he didn't want to. For show or not, being close to Cagney felt wonderful. Right. He took a moment to revel in her body pressed up against his, then muttered, "Here goes nothing," under his breath before he pulled open the door to Gulch Grapevine Central.

The bell jangled.

Everyone turned, purely by habit.

And conversation stopped.

Just for a few seconds, but long enough to tell them their entrance had been noticed and logged for rapid distribution via the vine as soon as possible. *Cagney Bishop and Jonas Eberhardt—no, I'm not kidding! I saw it with my own two eyes. They were all over each other.* You could count on small towns for a few things, and spreading the word was one of them.

Jonas slid his arm off of Cagney's shoulders and placed his hand at the small of her back, letting her guide them through the tables toward an empty one in the middle of everything. A perfect location for their purposes. It was a four-top, but they chose the two chairs closest to each other that faced the front of the restaurant. Instead of two menus, they put their heads together over a single one and tangled fingers as they discussed what to order in private, quiet tones. It might be pretend, but it felt real enough to Jonas that he didn't want it to end.

After all these years, Cagney was still a sucker for their pancake sandwich, he learned, but she was dithering over that and the day's special—huevos rancheros, which was apparently a great dish.

Jonas, having already decided on buckwheat pancakes, glanced up when the bell jangled. It really was a Pavlovian response, that darn bell. Three uniformed officers walked in and headed straight toward the take-out counter.

"Incoming," Jonas said, under his breath.

Cagney peered up, then sat straighter. "Oh, this is more perfect than I'd imagined." She grinned and waved when one of the younger officers, Mike Howell, glanced her way and did a double take. He hadn't been with TGPD long enough to know the sordid history between Cagney and her father yet, but the older officers had been on the job since she and Jonas were in high school. They knew the scoop. Howell waved back, then smacked Sergeant Roland Martinez in the arm patch and leaned in to say something. Roland did his own double take, then said something to the third officer.

"Scoot closer," Cagney rasped.

"What, you want me on your lap?" Jonas muttered in reply.

"They'll come over to say hi and dig for details, I promise. Just make it look like you ravished me last night."

He snorted. "What, you want me to mess

up the back of your hair and give you a quick hickey?"

She turned to glare at him playfully, then her expression changed, and she leaned in for a soft but powerful kiss.

The kiss didn't feel like an act.

The restaurant disappeared for him.

He heard nothing. Saw nothing. Smelled nothing.

Except Cagney.

When they tore away from each other, Officer Mike Howell, Sergeant Roland Martinez, and Senior Officer Chet Collins stood in a semicircle in front of their table.

Cagney started. "Oh, hey guys! You surprised me. Stealth approach—nice job." She stood, shook the two older officers' hands and gave Mike a quick hug. "Good to see you. You remember Jonas Eberhardt, don't you?" She laid a proprietary hand on his shoulder and introduced them one by one.

"'Course we do," Chet said in a formal and not altogether warm tone. "Nice to see you."

Jonas stood and shook the man's hand. "Likewise."

"I don't think we've met," Mike said, with an easy grin. "I'm the newbie of the group, hanging with the old dogs to learn some new tricks. But it's great what you're doing here in the Gulch. I've kept up on the progress of the new hospital wing in the newspaper."

"Don't forget the teen center," Cagney said.

"That, too," Howell added.

"Well, thanks. It's my pleasure to be back in the Gulch," Jonas said, deciding he liked Mike Howell already.

The sergeant stepped in and reached out for a firm handshake. "I have to second what Howell here says, Jonas." The salt-and-pepper-haired man swallowed back some emotion that made his eyes shine, though he remained stoic. "We just found out our four-year-old grandson, Armando, is autistic—"

"Oh, Sarge," Cagney said, splaying a hand on her chest. "I hadn't heard. I'm sorry."

Martinez pressed his lips together and nodded, then refocused on Jonas. "He's a great little guy. Just...." He cleared his throat. "His parents are still reeling from the diagnosis, but the wife and I think this art therapy idea might be able to pull him out of his shell some. He loves to paint and color, stuff like that. It eases his frustration level. This gives us hope, the new wing. I can't thank you enough for bringing it here. Our family wouldn't have had access to it otherwise."

"Best of luck to you. We look forward to meeting Armando once we open," Jonas said sincerely.

"Boys, your order's up," the waitress called across the dining room to the officers. She set a large white bag and a tray of coffee cups on the counter.

"We better go," Sergeant Martinez said. "Good to see you, Cagney. We've missed you out there."

"I've missed you guys, too," she said, surprised to realize that she meant it. "Stop by the teen center sometime soon to see how it's shaping up. And tell all the kids you contact about it."

"You two coming to the Policeman's Ball?" Mike asked, aiming a finger like a gun at her.

Cagney wrapped her arm around Jonas's biceps and leaned closer. "You bet we'll be there. See you then?"

Mike saluted, then followed the others toward the cash register in a loose-hipped swagger. Once they'd paid, waved and left, both Cagney and Jonas released simultaneous sighs

"That was tense," Jonas said. "And I don't know why. Everyone was nice enough."

"I think it's the 'coming out' aspect," Cagney said. "Mike and the Sarge are cool. But ol' Chet's in my father's back pocket, big-time."

"I know," Jonas said, grimly. "I remember him well from high school."

"He's not such a bad guy, really," Cagney said, taking a sip of the ice water one of the busboys had slipped onto the table while they'd been talking to her coworkers. "Chief leads the weaker ones along by their invisible nose rings. He takes advantage of the fact that they want to please him, rise up in the ranks. It's cruel, really."

"I don't care what ol' Chet thinks of me anyway, as long as he gets word back to Chief."

"Oh, you betcha he will. Probably on the cell phone as we speak."

Jonas slid his closed menu back into the metal holder at the edge of the table. "Well, as long as no one puts a hit on me between now and the ball," he said in a sardonic tone, "looks like our nefarious plan should work out."

Cagney smacked him in the arm. "Don't even *say* that." A line of worry bisected her forehead, and she wound her hands into a tight knot.

"Why the face? You can't possibly think something like that could happen. I was joking."

"No. I know." Cagney chewed on her bottom lip for a moment, then brightened. "I have a great idea, though." She adjusted in her chair and faced him head-on. "Give up your hotel suite in Crested Butte and move into my guest room."

"Are you nuts?" he asked, putting on a show of resisting, but inside he soared with joy. He hadn't realized he'd been waiting for some kind of invitation into her life until that moment.

"No, just listen. It's perfect." She lowered her tone. "No one has to know you're staying in the guest room rather than my room. And you won't have to make that late-night drive anymore after a long day's work."

He tucked his chin back. "Wait a minute. You *do* think he'd put a hit on me, don't you? Nab me late at night between here and Crested Butte, make it look like an accident?"

"I'm not saying that. He's a creep, but I don't think he's a cold-blooded—" She shook off the thought. "Your comment just sparked the idea, that's all. It'll serve our purposes perfectly and save you a drive you don't need to make. Win-win."

"Well…" He cocked his head to the side, pretending to consider it, even though he already knew he'd say yes. "It would shorten my commute."

She laughed. "Considerably."

"And Chief would burst a vein."

Her eyes sparkled. "Indubitably."

A pause, followed by a shrug. "What the heck? I'm getting tired of room service anyway, and apparently you cook a mean elk steak." He smiled.

She cocked her eyebrow. "You expect me to cook for you?"

"I don't know if I'd use the word *expect*." He winked. "But I'd be very grateful. *Very*."

She scoffed at his blatant flirting. "I'm only kidding. I love cooking, and I can only lure my friends over once a month. It's like they have lives of their own. What's *that* about?" She shook her head at the insanity of it all. "It'll be a pleasure to prepare meals for more than just one person every night. So, we have a deal?"

"You'll have to let me pay you."

"Don't be insulting." She leaned closer and widened her eyes. "We're in the midst of a torrid affair, remember?"

Whatever. He just wanted to be close to Cagney. "You let me buy all the groceries, and we have a deal."

"How can I say no to that?" She threw her arms around him and they kissed again, then remained forehead to forehead, just staring into each other's eyes.

Jonas wondered if it was for show on her part.

As for him, he'd never been happier, and though he'd play it the way she wanted, inside none of this was for anyone in the Gulch except Cagney. And himself. That might wind up destroying him in the end, but he was going to enjoy the present for as long as it lasted.

Not that he'd let her know how he truly felt. "You're beautiful," he said, his tone husky.

"Please. I already said I'd cook for you. You can cut the gratuitous flattery." She lowered her tone to a conspiratorial whisper. "I don't think anyone's listening."

"No," he said, not latching on to her attempt to lighten things up. "I mean it. You're the most beautiful woman I've ever known in my life. Inside and out."

"Aw, Jonas." Her luscious mouth spread into a slow smile. "Thank you."

"Um, get a room?" came a whispered suggestion right by their ears.

They wrenched apart to find Faith standing there grinning. She aimed a finger at Cagney. "*So* going to kill you for holding out on me, girl. A painful death, too."

"Faith, what are you doing here?"

"I got a call from Brody who got a call from Mike Howell that you and the new guy in town were hot and heavy at the Pinecone. The Pinecone! Of all places. Had to run down from the high school and check out the rumor for myself."

Jonas widened his eyes at Cagney.

She shrugged. "I told you. The grapevine is an amazing and incomprehensible thing."

"So, what's the word?" Faith asked, reaching out to thunk Cagney on the forehead with her finger.

"Ow!" Cagney rubbed the spot. "Not here, okay? Can you and Brody come over for dinner tonight? Jonas is staying at my place from now on—"

"Is he, now?" She narrowed her eyes at her friend. "Glad I had to hear it through the grapevine."

"It's sudden. We'll explain everything tonight."

"Brody's on a twenty-four-hour shift," Faith said, tapping a finger on her chin. "So's Erin. But Lexy's off and Nate's in town…I think. In any case, I'll activate the phone tree, and whoever can come will be there. I'll make sure. Seven?"

"Perfect," Cagney said.

Faith leaned in and gave Jonas a big, noisy smackeroo on the cheek. "Welcome back, sweetheart. It's about time."

Jonas watched the woman who bore an uncanny resemblance to her older sister wind her way out of the restaurant, wondering if this situation could possibly get more complicated.

In the end, only Faith and Lexy were free for dinner. Even Jonas had to run off and take care of some construction problem at the hospital, but somehow, Cagney was relieved that he'd left. She needed some alone time with her girlfriends to talk through her unexpected surge of feelings.

Ever since she and Jonas had agreed to their plan, he had been attentive and affectionate in and out of public, always claiming it was for "practice." But when he'd told her she was beautiful at the diner…and when he'd rubbed her feet after their workday…and when he'd pulled her body against his for a kiss that left her shaky and aching before he went to the hospital that evening, well, it just didn't feel like practice.

It felt like destiny.

And he seemed like the old Jonas, only better.

Most surprising, *she* felt like painting again. Colors and ideas and that fire-in-the-belly urge to create overtook her until she found herself digging her easel out of a back closet and setting it up in a spot before one of her north-facing windows. She touched each one of her brushes, even squished some paint out onto her ancient color-covered palette, just to marvel in its infinite, beautiful possibilities.

A major seismic shift was occurring in her life, and she didn't know quite what to make of it. She needed her friends.

She whipped up a quick, one-pan, garbanzo-bean-and-chorizo dish they all loved, then they settled into the living room with wine. Lexy raised herself out of her wheelchair with her upper body and claimed the down-filled chair-and-a-half that had been a steal at a consignment shop in Steamboat Springs. She used both hands to lift one leg after the other and tuck them beneath her, cross-legged. Sitting that way, she almost looked like a fully able-bodied young woman, which struck Cagney as poignant.

She and Faith claimed opposite ends of the sofa, stretching their legs out to tangle their feet. They'd talked about their workdays, current television topics and clothes, but the subject of her and Jonas hadn't come up. Until now.

"Okay, we've waited long enough," Faith said, with classic Montesantos female bluntness. "Last night you and Jonas were at each other's throats, today you're sucking face in the Pinecone. What cosmic occurrence did we miss in the past twenty-four hours?"

So Cagney told them everything. When she was done, she glanced from one friend to the other, waiting for a reaction.

"That's such bull," Faith said.

Okay, unexpected. "What? You think we're making a mistake?"

"No. I understand your need to get back at Chief. We think you're fooling yourselves, though," Lexy replied.

Cagney pulled back her chin. "In what way? Mike Howell believed Jonas and I enough to call Brody the instant he left the Pinecone this morning. I think we're pulling it off."

Faith laughed, shaking her head and raising her eyebrows at Lexy. "Clueless."

"No doubt," Lexy said.

Cagney spread her arms wide. "What?"

"You're not *pulling anything off,* doofus," Faith told her. "You're *in love.* You and Jonas, and it's meant to be. Anyone can see it."

"Well, anyone but them," Lexy said. She winked at Cagney. "Some weird need for revenge might have brought Jonas back to the Gulch, but fate has kept him here."

After a brief pause, Cagney groaned and laid her head back against the cushions. "Okay, yes, I do love him. Crazy love. I want him in my bed, not my guest room. I want him in my life every day until…forever, because we've lost so much time already, and I've always loved him." She sighed morosely. "But that's not part of our—"

"Let me guess," Faith said, wryly. "Not part of your deal. Your plan. Your grand scheme."

Cagney eyed her stubbornly.

"When are the two of you going to stop making deals and start admitting that you want to be together?"

"I'm afraid." Cagney bit her bottom lip.

"Afraid of what?" Lexy asked, gently.

"Afraid I'm in love and he really is just fully signed on with the plan. Nothing else."

"Argh!" Faith shook her head. "If Mick were here right now, Cag, she'd smack you."

Cagney's eyes widened. "Mick never smacked me."

"Well, she would now. Being a guardian angel gives you certain rights and privileges. And she'd tell you, like Lex and I are telling you, take a *risk,* honey," Faith pleaded. "Let go of your fear. I will clean this loft by hand every week for the rest of our lives if that man isn't in love with you." She crossed her heart.

"Faith's right," Lexy said.

"I'll try. I am trying," Cagney said. "But, I can't think about that yet. First things first. Do you think our plan is going to work?"

Faith frowned. "To piss off Chief?"

"Oh, definitely," Lexy said. "And I'm going to be there to witness it."

Cagney straightened. "You're coming to the Police Ball?"

"Yes."

"With a date?"

"Of course not," Lexy said, averting her

gaze for a moment. "I've volunteered to work at the event, taking tickets, that sort of thing. I do it every couple of years."

"You do?" Cagney asked, baffled. "How come I never knew that?"

Lexy shrugged. "I didn't want you to think I was there with the rest of them, kissing your father's ring, so to speak. It's just a way for me to give back and stay in touch with the officers."

Cagney smiled. "You could've told me. I understand."

"Well, now you know."

Cagney untangled her feet from Faith's and stood up to go give Lexy a hug, but just then the freight elevator opened, and Jonas stepped off. He smiled easily at the women. "Hello, ladies. I trust dinner was enjoyable?"

"Cagney's the best cook in town," Faith said.

He crossed to Cagney then, until no space remained between their bodies. "Honey, I'm home," he teased, tilting his head down to look into her eyes. Unmindful of their audience, he slipped all ten fingers into her hair, cradling her head, then gave her a kiss that left them all holding their breath. When he pulled back, he winked at Lexy and Faith.

"Practice makes perfect, they say. Gotta be convincing. Right, Cag?"

"Uh." She couldn't think. "D-do you want…um…"

"Cag," Faith prodded.

Cagney cleared her throat. "Do you want some dinner?"

"Love some." He aimed a thumb toward the elevator. "I'll just run upstairs and wash up, and I'll be back down in a minute."

"Use the guest powder room," Cagney said, distractedly. "It's just on the other side of the kitchen."

He reached out and stroked her chin gently. "Thanks."

Once he was out of the main room, Cagney wheeled around and big-eyed her friends in question and panic, equally mixed.

"That," Faith said smugly, "was *not* for practice."

Cagney clasped her necklace in her fist. "Are you sure?"

"She's sure," Lexy said, grinning. "And so am I. Admit it, so are you."

"Okay. I am, I think. But what do I do?" Cagney whispered, shaking her hands as if she'd burned them.

"Go for it!" her friends said in unison.

Chapter Ten

As the week before the dance dragged on, Cagney tried to focus on the plan, but she couldn't stop obsessing about the letter Chief had given to Jonas on prom night. She'd retrieved it from the floor of the teen center the morning after he'd shown it to her, and every time she reread it, the resentment toward her mother grew.

She didn't want to be estranged from both her parents.

Something had to give.

On Thursday, Jonas had to be away all evening dealing with hospital issues, and her father—Cagney knew—would be stuck at the city council meeting until late into the night. Midmorning, when she knew her father wouldn't be there, she called her parents' house. After three rings, her mother, Helen, answered.

"Hey, Mom," Cagney said, in a flat tone.

"Cagney! This is a nice surprise, honey. What's up?"

Cagney clenched the phone receiver tighter. She wished this could be more of a social call, especially when Mom sounded so thrilled to hear from her, but the swirl of bitterness in her middle made it something else. "I was wondering if you'd come over for dinner tonight. I know Chief will be working late, and there's something I want to talk to you about. Alone."

"Why, I'd love to," her mom said, so pleased it made Cagney's heart clench. "Will it just be you and me?"

"Yes."

"How nice," Helen said, her genuine excitement humming across the phone line, as though she'd been invited to an all-girls spa weekend rather than a simple dinner.

An unexpected sting of tears made Cagney close her eyes. Her mom hadn't been the strongest of women, but still. Angry at the moment or not, Cagney should've included her in her own life more often. If she had, they might have a better relationship now.

"Should I bring anything?" her mom asked.

A damn good explanation. Cagney cleared the emotion out of her throat. "Nope. Just you. Is six okay?"

"Perfect. I can't wait. See you then, honey."

They'd made small talk over dinner and dessert, and it wasn't until they were enjoying cups of coffee that the subject came up.

"So, I hear you and Jonas are back together," her mom said lightly, straightening out some imaginary wrinkles in her slacks and avoiding Cagney's gaze.

"Yes," Cagney said in a harder-than-necessary tone. "Is that a problem?"

Helen lifted one thin shoulder. "Not for me."

Cagney waited out her mom's pause.

"I may have never said it, but I always liked that boy. And his poor mother." She shook her head. "I would have reached out to her, that's how I was raised. But your father…" The lines around her eyes seemed to deepen. She sipped her coffee.

Her father. *Always* her father.

Cagney huffed with frustration. "If you'd wanted to reach out and befriend Ava Eberhardt, you should've. Why do you let him control you, Mom? Why did you let him control all of us?"

Helen's chin quivered, and she gazed off in the distance, past Cagney. "Oh, honey." She sighed, finally meeting her eyes. "I was never taught to defy my husband. I know it's not much of an excuse for women of your generation. I do realize I wasn't a good role model for you girls. Don't think I'm blind to that."

Cagney felt a pang of compassion for her mom, who seemed so old right then, so world-weary. Her emotional roller-coaster cart hit the bottom of a big hill, lurched, then started that slow crank upward again. "You did the best you could, I suppose."

"I tried."

Moment of truth. "I have to ask you something, Mom." Cagney's heart started to pound.

"Okay."

Taking a deep breath, she pulled the fragile

piece of paper Jonas had carried with him all these years from her pocket, and slid it toward her mom without a single word of explanation.

Helen's pale blue eyes scanned it, then filled with tears. One of them dropped onto the page, smearing a single purple line. She sniffed and glanced up. "Casey Laine, I'm more sorry about that note than anything else in my life."

Cagney's gut spasmed. "So you did write it."

"Yes. Against my will."

Cagney scraped her chair back abruptly and paced to the window. She stared out, trying to get her anger in check, then turned back toward her mother, arms crossed. "Why, Mom? How could you let him destroy your own daughter's life like that? I am so…furious with you right now, I don't even know what else to say."

Quiet tears coursed down Helen Bishop's face, but she didn't bother to wipe them away. "I don't know what to say, either. No explanation will make this letter disappear, sweetheart. I've regretted giving in to his pressure to write that thing since the day it happened. But your father…he's a calculating man—"

"He's a monster!" Cagney said in a burst of rage. "He drove Terri away, destroyed my life. He turned Deirdre into some kind of a clone, and look at you." She flicked her hand. "He's had you running scared for almost forty years. When will it all stop? When are you going to stand up to him?"

Helen sighed. "I'm not as strong as you girls."

"Strong?" Cagney choked out a humorless laugh. "We don't even have a real family, Mom. I never see you because of him. I don't even know my own sisters anymore. None of us are strong, because we've let him dictate the way we live. We don't even talk openly about everything that's wrong and toxic in our family. Why is that?"

Helen stood then, brushed the tears from her face and held her chin high. She crossed to Cagney and took her hand, leading her to the couch. "Come on. Take a deep breath. Sit with me."

Strangely, Cagney found comfort in her mother acting like a parent for once. They shuffled to the couch side-by-side, then sat. By then, Cagney's anger demanded release, and she'd begun to cry.

Helen pressed one of Cagney's hands

between her own. "I'm going to ask for a favor I don't deserve, and then we're going to air out some dirty laundry once and for all."

Cagney gulped. "Okay."

"First, the favor. Can you ever forgive me for the note?" her mother implored. "I realize I should have stood stronger against your father's threats, but—"

"Wait a minute. He threatened you, too?" Cagney said, her eyes narrowing. "You wrote the note because he threatened you?"

"Yes."

"Why did he threaten *you?*"

Her mom huffed out a sad sound, almost like a laugh, but not quite there. "Because I stood up for you and Jonas that night, before the prom. I told him I thought he was misjudging the boy, and that he should let the two of you go together."

Cagney's chest squeezed until she saw stars. "Y-you did?"

Helen nodded. "That set him off like I'd never seen before. We had quite the row, and he backed me into a corner, Cagney." She pressed her lips together. "He told me if I didn't write the note, that, among other things, he wouldn't send you to college—"

"Oh, my God, Mom. He used the same threat with me."

Little hot spots of anger rose to Helen's cheeks. "You know your father controls the household finances. Still does, to this day. Things would've been different if I'd had any money of my own. At least, I like to think so…."

"No, it's okay. It's your money, too, even though he earns it. That's what marriage is. A team."

"You'd think so."

Cagney scooted closer and rested her head on her mom's shoulder. "I know what a trap his threats can be, controlling bastard that he is. I just wish you'd have told me."

"How can you tell your daughter something like that?"

"You just…do. I don't know."

"I probably would've found a way after prom night." Helen pressed her warm cheek against the top of Cagney's head. "But after the accident, the whole incident faded. I just wanted you home and healthy. I almost couldn't bear for you to be out of my sight," her voice cracked. She cleared her throat and went on. "I watched you sleep every night for months after that."

"Really? I didn't know."

Her mom nodded against her head. "And by the time you'd been released from the hospital, Jonas was gone anyway…" She trailed off, on a sigh. "I'm making excuses, and poor ones at that. I should've told you. You're right." And then, in a softer voice, "Can you forgive me?"

"Of course." Cagney sighed. "I love you, Mom. I just wish…."

"I know. I wish a lot of things, too." She gave Cagney a squeeze. "But look at the bright side. Jonas is back, the two of you have reconciled, and you're adults. There's not a blessed thing your father can do about it."

But they'd lost so much time, Cagney thought wistfully. "Why is Chief such an angry person?" She sat up, then turned to sit cross-legged and face her mother directly.

"Well," Helen said with a sigh, "your father's suffered through his share of traumas."

"So he chooses to inflict them on others? Great logic." Cagney unfolded her legs and retrieved their coffee mugs, then rejoined her mom on the sofa.

"I know. He hasn't dealt with things the

best he could, but that's your father." Helen brushed her fingers through her bobbed blond and gray hair. "You know how we never talked about your Grandma Bishop?"

Cagney nodded. "Because she died when Chief was young, right?"

"Well, that was your father's story."

Utter shock zinged through Cagney, rocking her world. "His *story?* Grandma's not dead?"

Helen shook her head. "Dead to him, maybe. But the reality is, she's alive and mostly well. In prison."

"What?" Cagney rasped.

"It's a sad, sordid tale, honey. A tragedy all the way around. If you don't want to hear it—"

"No. No. There's been enough hiding in the Bishop household. Tell me everything."

Helen sipped her coffee, then set it on the end table. She turned to sit cross-legged like Cagney, folding her hands together in her lap. "When your father was just a small boy, Grandpa Bishop worked as a guard at the men's prison in Cañon City."

"Yes, I knew that part."

"Well, Grandma Bishop was a social worker there. They had a very high-profile murderer come into the facility when your father was, oh, about four years old, and Leila—that's your grandma's name—"

"Leila," Cagney repeated softly.

"—well, she was assigned to counsel the man," her mom continued.

"How scary."

"I agree. Most people would think so,. at least." Helen shook her head. "Anyway, the man was a charmer as so many of those sociopaths are—"

"Like Ted Bundy."

"Yes. And Leila fell in love with him."

Cagney braced herself on the cushion between her and her mother with both palms. "Are you serious? My grandma is one of those infamous women who fell for an inmate?"

Helen twisted her mouth to the side. "Unfortunately, yes. More infamous than you've ever known."

"In what way?"

"After she and this murderer were caught, well, together in her office, the sordid tale ripped through the prison. She was fired, of course, and your grandpa never quite got past the shame and bitterness. Grandma declared her love for the inmate, divorced your grandpa, and he was down on women from that day forward."

"A trait he lovingly passed on to Chief."

"That, he did."

"Wow. I'm so…blown away." Cagney eased out a breath. "So what happened to Grandma?"

"She and this murderer were married in one of those awful prison ceremonies—"

"No!"

"Yes, and a few years later, he somehow brainwashed her to try and help him escape."

"From Territorial Prison? Good luck," Cagney said, remembering the time she'd toured the supermax prison with the county diversion program.

Helen nodded. "It's a sad story, really. Security wasn't as tight then. They got pretty far with their plans, but the guards shot him during the escape attempt, and in her anguish, Grandma Leila shot at the guards."

Cagney gasped.

Helen wound both of her hands into fists and knocked them on her thighs. "I have to believe Leila wasn't a criminal, but rather a young, manipulated woman who got caught up in things way beyond her."

Cagney swallowed. "Did she…kill the guard?"

Helen splayed a palm on her chest. "No. Thank goodness. But she was convicted of attempted murder and a slew of other things. She's been in the women's prison in Florissant ever since." Helen picked up a throw pillow and hugged it to her lap, fingering the fringe absentmindedly. "Your father grew up hearing how women couldn't be trusted, how women fell for bad men, on and on—you can just imagine."

"Then, how did you two end up together?"

"I was different in his eyes, I guess. You know the kind of strict, religious background I was raised in."

"Yes."

"And I had wonderful parents, devoted to each other and to their church." She shrugged. "I guess your father felt I was a safe bet, that I'd never leave him, especially not for a criminal."

"But come on. What are the odds of that? Grandma Leila's situation was a fluke."

"Oh, I know. It's probably hard to believe, but he and I had a pretty good marriage the first couple years."

"I can't even imagine it. But I believe you." Cagney tucked her hair behind her ears. "What changed it?"

"Having three daughters." Helen twisted her mouth to the side. "Suddenly, all his fears rose to the surface again. He could only see danger on the horizon for all of you. Eventually that fear reacted like a poison in his body until he could only be…well, the man you know. It affects everything he does with our family."

"That's so unfair. Doesn't he realize how much joy and life he missed out on with his kids? None of us were screwups. Not even Terri."

"No, Terri's no screwup," her mother said softly.

"But how can you stand it?"

"Oh, believe me, we've had our blowout arguments over the whole thing."

"You and Chief? I never heard you fight."

Helen smiled sadly. "I wasn't raised to fight in front of the children. Maybe I should've."

"Or maybe Chief should have reacted like a sane man," Cagney said with a huff.

"I'm not saying he reacted logically," Helen conceded, angling her chin down. "Just telling you how it was."

"I guess it makes a twisted kind of sense. It just makes me so mad that he acts like Mr.

Upstanding Lawman in public when he's something else altogether, and all the clueless guys worship him as this perfect cop. The ultimate man." She flexed her biceps. "Strong."

"Some of them see through it, Cagney."

She wanted to ask which ones, but instead, she crossed her arms. "So? They still suck up."

"Well, that's because he's the boss, not because they think he's a model citizen. You're in the field, honey. You know how it is with those who want to move through the ranks."

"I guess. I don't like it, but I get it." Cagney leaned back against the sofa arm and exhaled. "Wow, this is just…so much to take in. My own father thought his daughters would grow up to be idiots, so he ruined all our lives. And I descend from a line of criminals. Great."

"Your descendents are not criminals," Helen said firmly. "Leila made some bad choices and a few huge, life-changing mistakes, for sure. Who hasn't made mistakes, though?"

Cagney looked at her with skepticism. "Mom, there are mistakes, and then there's marrying a murderer and trying to bust him out of prison, shooting at a guard, going to—"

"I understand that," Helen said, holding up a palm. "But the world has judged her enough, don't you think? And she'll be judged again when she passes."

A niggle of guilt poked at Cagney. "You're right, I guess."

"She's alone in prison, she's elderly, and to top it all off, she's showing early stages of Alzheimer's," Helen said with an air of true knowledge. "She's paying the price for her crimes without you and I judging her, too."

Cagney could hardly take in a full breath. "Wait a minute. You've visited her?"

"Not visited. I could never explain a trip like that to your father." Her mom hesitated, tipping her head to the side. "But I do send her a care package every so often. Just a few nice things to ease her loneliness and a prayer or two."

"Mom, that's really sweet of you."

Helen shrugged. "We're two women suffering for our choices in men. I've been in my own kind of prison. And she *is* my mother-in-law, after all. I don't condone her actions, but I can't stand by coldly and imagine her sorrow and isolation without doing something about it."

"You're a good, good person, Mama,"

Cagney said, leaning forward to hold her mom's hands. "I was so angry. I haven't been fair to you."

"None of that matters. You're my daughter, and I could've been a much better mother. We all do the best we can on this earth, and there's not much more beyond that. What do you say we do a better job of being mother and daughter from here on out?"

"I'd love that," Cagney said, warmth spreading through her.

Helen glanced up at the wall clock. "I should get home, though, much as I don't want to leave. I'd like to be there before your father is. I don't want to face an interrogation."

"What? You're not allowed to have dinner with your daughter?"

"No, it's just...I want this dinner to be mine," Helen said, smiling sadly. "Can you understand that? I don't want to share it with him."

Cagney studied her mom's face for several long moments, thinking Helen Bishop was stronger than she gave herself credit for. She nailed her with a pleading look. "Grandma Leila has to stay in her prison, Mom. You don't."

"I know. It's talk for another day, hmm?" She leaned forward and kissed Cagney on the cheek.

Cagney wrapped her in a hug, not wanting to let go. "Thank you for coming. For explaining things."

They broke apart, and Helen's eyes shone with unshed tears. "I should've talked to you a long time ago, come clean about that letter."

Cagney flicked her hand. "Bygones. I just wish you had a happier life, Mom. I wish there were something I could do."

"It's not for you to do. It's on me, this one." Helen smiled, looking more at peace than Cagney had seen her for a long time. She laid one cool palm against Cagney's cheek. "I'm okay, Casey Laine. But you…you go out there and be happy, my sweet girl. That's the gift you can give me and yourself. Jonas is a good man, and the two of you deserve each other and every one of life's happy moments. You have my blessing."

Cagney stood and walked her mom to the elevator in silence. They'd shared a rare evening of honesty…she didn't have the heart to tell her the so-called reconciliation was all for show.

* * *

The day before the Police Ball, Jonas had surprised her with an absolutely stunning floor-length black beaded mermaid style gown and shoes to match. It fit perfectly and made her feel like a fairy princess.

This was way better than the prom would've been.

Lexy had come over to help her with her hair and makeup and had just left to get dressed herself. Cagney was loading a few essentials into an evening bag when she heard the freight elevator open on her floor. She smiled.

"Oh, Cinderella? Prince Not-So-Charming is here to pick you up for the ball," Jonas called out.

She shook her head. "I'm back here."

"Back where?" She could hear his footsteps on the hardwood floors. "Marco?"

"Polo," she answered, laughing. "In my bedroom."

The footsteps stopped. "I'll wait for you out here."

"Chicken," she teased.

"A gentleman waits for a lady to make an entrance, Cagney," he said with playful righteous indignation.

"Okay, Mr. Manners. Be there in a sec." She snapped her satin bag shut and took one last look at herself in the mirror. Lexy had styled her hair in a free-flowing upsweep with loose tendrils that floated against her cheeks and nape. Her makeup looked better than it ever had when she applied it herself, with dark smoky eyes and natural lips. Jonas had always preferred natural lips to the lined and lipsticked variety.

Sexy Lexy had some serious skills. Turning this way and that, Cagney could hardly believe the woman in the mirror was her. She actually looked like a girl!

The guys at work would freak. She grinned.

Picking up her small clutch, she took a deep breath and headed out into the living room.

Jonas, who'd been perusing a book from her library shelves turned when he heard her stiletto heels on the floor. He froze, and the book fell from his hands.

"Wow! That's the best reaction I've ever gotten from a guy." Cagney, feeling playful, twirled in a circle. "Either your hands are really tired or I pass inspection."

Jonas stooped to retrieve the book, but his eyes never left her face, except to trace her body in a way that made her heart pound. "You more than pass inspection, Cag," he said in a husky tone. "I knew that dress would be perfect with your blond hair."

It took him three tries to get the book re-shelved.

Cagney laughed, taking a moment to study Jonas. He looked impeccable and delicious in his tailor-made tux. Good enough to eat, that was for sure. "You look wonderful, too, Jonas."

"Who cares about me? I'm the guy." He crossed the room as though mesmerized and gently cupped her chin. His gaze dropped to her lips, and he smiled.

"I remembered," she said, breathlessly.

"I see that." He leaned in for a kiss.

She opened her mouth to him, inhaling his skin and reveling in the moment. When he pulled away, she uttered a sound of protestation and tried to tug him back toward her.

"Hang on. I have something for you."

She clapped her hands. "A prom corsage!"

"No, I don't have fondness for prom corsages." He extracted a small, white cardboard box from his inside jacket pocket. "I was going to give you this on prom night."

She sucked in a breath and laid a palm on her chest. "Oh, Jonas."

"It's nothing, trust me. But at the time, it had taken me six months to save up for, so it was a big deal then." He thrust the box closer. "Open it."

She did so, with shaky hands. Inside lay a sterling silver charm bracelet with just two charms: an artist's palette and one half of a soul mates medallion. A lump rose in her throat. "It's…perfect. It couldn't be more perfect."

"Here, let me put it on you."

After he'd clasped it, she twisted her arm in the air in front of her, jangling the charms.

"I'd planned on getting you more charms eventually."

"Where's the other half—?"

He lifted up his sleeve to display a thicker men's chain bracelet, with the other half of the soul mate medallion attached.

She sighed. "You're incredible. I can't believe you kept it all this time."

"You know, me neither."

"Thank you."

He held up a finger. "Wait, there's more."

"What are you talking about? You're a nut."

He slipped his hand into the other side of his jacket and extracted a long, black velvet box. "That was a gift for back then, what we missed." He paused. "This is a gift for now."

Cagney's heart was pounding so wildly, she couldn't speak. She snapped open the box and found the most brilliant diamond choker she'd ever seen. She gasped, blinking up at him.

"It's perfect with the dress. Plus, it'll look right." He shrugged. "A man in love would shower his lady with trinkets and baubles. It's in the code."

Cagney wasn't sure what to make of that, but it seemed to be one piece of evidence to chalk up on the just-for-show side. Her stomach tightened. "This is no trinket, Jonas. It's amazing."

"I'm glad you like it. Let's put it on." He took the box back from her, and she turned away from him.

Cagney blinked rapidly, unsure if this was a gift or a loaner. But from what he said…

"All secure."

She turned back, resting her hand on the cool ring of diamonds. "Thank you. I promise not to lose it or damage it so you can return it when we're done with this."

His eyes shadowed in confusion. "Return it?"

"Well, you said that stuff about it looking right for a guy supposedly in love…."

"Cagney, that's not what I meant. The necklace is for you. To keep."

After a moment, she stood on tiptoe and kissed him gently. "You don't have to buy me expensive gifts. That's not what this is about."

He ran the back of his hand down her cheek. "I know. I wanted to buy it for you."

She shook her head, then laughed nervously. "I'll turn quite a few heads at the Pinecone in this thing. Thank you."

"Well, I hope you'll have other places to wear it besides the Pinecone." He flicked his wrist and checked his watch. "We should go."

Now or never.

"Jonas?" she asked, in a soft tone, stopping him just as he turned toward the console table adjacent to the elevator door where he'd dropped his car keys.

"Mmm-hmm?"

"What are the odds this thing could stick?"

His baffled expression moved from her

face to the diamond choker. "What do you mean? The clasp?"

"No," she said, boldly. "This thing between you and me."

Their gazes tangled again, and her heart started to drum. She'd die if he shot her down. She realized they had the whole showdown at the Not-Okay Corral to deal with, but she wanted him to say it. Flat out. Either way, she needed to know right then and there.

He reached out and took her hand in his, gently massaging her silky soft knuckles. "Let's take one step at a time, honey. Okay? Tonight's going to be—"

"I understand." She leaned her body into his, hopefully making her intentions clear. "I just want you to know—"

He laid a finger across her lips. "I do know."

She maneuvered her hand over so she could squeeze his, and gave him one of her sunbeam-breaking-through-clouds smiles. She thought about the little extra surprise she had in store for Chief. "I'm glad you're here, Jonas."

He leaned in and kissed her forehead. "I

am, too, honey. And I never thought I'd say those words."

"Amazing what a few months and some honest conversation can change, huh?"

"I'll say. But first things first. How about you and I go lay some old bones to rest. Infuriating Chief?" He leaned in and nipped her bottom lip with this teeth. "Sounds like some pretty intense foreplay, if you ask me."

Chapter Eleven

Troublesome Gulch Ski Lodge had hosted
the Police Ball for as long as Cagney could
remember, probably because it was the only
business in the Gulch with a large enough—
and formal enough—great room. Still, the
Police Union had gone all out transforming
the place into as festive and glamorous a
setting as possible since this was their
biggest fund-raiser of the year. The old
familiar ski lodge was nearly unrecogniz-
able.

They'd festooned every tree, bush and
fence on the landscape with thousands of

white, twinkling lights, and a blue (in homage to the fact that this was a police event) carpet had been rolled out over the sidewalk. It really had turned out beautifully.

Still, Cagney couldn't let herself become completely dazzled by it. She took a deep, steadying breath as they pulled into the circle drive for valet parking, fighting her overactive nerves. She rubbed her palms together, noticing they'd grown moist. And morgue cold.

Jonas reached over and squeezed her shoulder. "You ready for this?"

She flashed him a quick, fake smile. "I am. More ready than you know. But I still have butterflies." She laid a palm on her abdomen. "And clammy hands—attractive, I know. Par for the course, I guess."

"For sure. We can leave whenever you're ready," he said soothingly. "Just say the word when you've done what you came to do, okay? This night is for you. For us." He pulled a face. "Frankly, I have no interest in hanging out with a bunch of cops for any longer than we have to. Well, except for one particular cop," he said in a sexy tone.

As attracted as she was to Jonas, her brain simply wasn't in that lusty mind set yet. She had a few hurdles to jump, an agenda she couldn't table until a later date. She'd waited long enough already. "Thank you," she said. "A lot of them are nice guys, though, Jonas. I hope you don't judge them all based on Chief and his cronies."

He seemed to concede the point. "I try not to judge people at all since I've been so misjudged myself." He hiked one shoulder. "Try and often fail—I'm not a total success story, by any stretch of the imagination. I did like that Mike Howell guy."

"Yeah, he's cool. Anyway, we won't stay long. I just want to see and be seen, show off my smokin' hot date." A pause. "And speak with my father. After that, I'm more than happy to leave."

Jonas raised his eyebrows. "You're actually going to talk to the guy?"

She nodded, firmly. "I have to. No, I want to. Don't worry, though. This time, I have the upper hand and an ironclad plan for maintaining that position. For once, I'm actually looking forward to a run-in with Chief."

Jonas opened his mouth as if to ask a question, but the valet approached, interrupting their conversation. He took Jonas's keys and a ten-dollar tip Jonas offered, then handed him a salmon-colored ticket, which Jonas slipped into the inside pocket of his jacket.

"Ready?" he asked.

"As I'm ever going to be."

They stepped onto the carpet-covered sidewalk, and Jonas offered his arm. She wrapped her hand around it gratefully, leaning closer. "This is our night, Jonas. A chance to reverse our fortune."

"A new beginning," he added.

"Definitely. So, for however long we're here, let's concentrate on making it memorable."

He leaned closer and kissed her temple. "You got it, sweetheart. I'm following your lead."

The music pounded as they entered the dimly lit and lavishly decorated room. Within moments, coworkers swarmed around Cagney, wolf-whistling and ogling her as she knew they would in that killer dress of hers. She basked in their appreciation and accepted their big bear hugs graciously, introducing Jonas to everyone as her boyfriend. The announcement fazed no one, but then again, these were her contemporaries, not her father's. A whirlwind of laughter and catching up engulfed them in those first few minutes.

Jonas, slightly out of the loop, whispered in her ear that he was going to the bar, then drifted away to get them each a glass of wine. She needed one, but hated to be away from him. While he was gone, everyone else moved on to mingle, one by one, until Cagney suddenly found herself alone. Like a target for Chief's arrows.

Goose bumps washed over her exposed skin as self-doubt took over. Engulfed in vulnerablity, she scoped out the area for Lexy but couldn't seem to find her. She hadn't been at the front taking tickets as they'd expected. Where was she?

"Here you go," Jonas said, returning to her side.

She spun and smiled up at him with relief, taking her glass. Thank God he was back. "You rock."

"Who were you looking for? Chief?" He took a sip of his drink.

"Not yet. Lexy, actually. And my mom."

Jonas raised one eyebrow. "She comes to these?"

"Oh, yes," Cagney said wryly. "Under duress, I'm sure. The woman behind the man, all that trumped up drivel."

"Gotcha." Jonas turned and scanned the

area, too, taking advantage of his extra height. "I don't see your mom, but there's Lexy," he said, pointing. "She's dancing with Howell."

"Ah, should've known." Cagney craned her neck to watch. "Poor Mike's had the hots for her forever."

"Understandable. She's a doll, just like always."

Cagney nodded, then they watched her for a few moments.

Jonas whistled softly. "Damn. She's a better dancer in a wheelchair than I am with my two left feet."

Cagney laughed. "Lexy was always an amazing dancer. She didn't give up much when she lost use of her legs. She's just that kind of resilient, you know?"

"That's a good thing. I'm sure her dating life hasn't suffered much, either."

Cagney took a gulp of wine. "Oh, Lex has all the interest she always did. Witness, Mike Howell's continued devotion. But she rebuffs it all."

"Why?"

"Well, in Mike's case, I don't think she's into him romantically. But she's a sweet girl who would never say no to a dance."

"What about other guys?"

Cagney shook her head. "The fact remains, Lexý Cabrera doesn't date, period."

Jonas looked perplexed. "I don't get it."

Cagney shrugged, swaying slightly to the music. "Simple. She knows she caused Randy to lose control of the SUV on prom night. I'm not blaming her—she blames herself. It's just a fact of what happened."

"How did it happen exactly? If you're okay talking about it."

"I am. Lexy was climbing onto Randy's lap as he drove, just being daring, playful Lexy, and her hip hit the wheel."

He blew out a breath. "That's a lot of weight on one soul."

Cagney nodded. "Just my theory, but I think she doesn't feel she deserves to fall in love, or even date, because of that. Guilt, you know? It's such an insidious thing."

"Such a shame. It could've happened to anyone." He shrugged. "Looking back, we were all basically idiots when we were teens. I think it's required."

"So sadly true." Cagney twisted her mouth to the side. "She swears she only needs her work to be happy, but come on. Doesn't everyone need somebody?"

"Allegedly," he said in a droll tone. "My friend, Kelli, has been telling me that for years."

Cagney looked at him sharply, irritated with herself when an uncharacteristic swirl of jealousy flipped her stomach. She tore her gaze away, still rocking to the beat of the band, albeit a bit more stiffly. After a few moments of silence, she cleared her throat, unable to refrain. "So, what kind of friend is this Kelli?"

Jonas set his drink on a nearby pub table and pulled her against him. "Do I detect a jealous vibe?" he teased.

"It was just a question," she said—peevishly because she'd been busted. She hiked her chin, a meager attempt to hold on to her dwindling self-esteem.

He leaned down and kissed her softly. "Kelli is the kind of friend who is marrying my best buddy, Tony."

"Oh," she said, feeling small and stupid.

"They've been head over heels since all of us were in college. Not to worry."

"I'm not worried," Cagney said, a little too quickly.

Jonas grinned. "Uh-huh."

"Be quiet, Jonas. I'm embarrassed enough as it is."

"Kel just thinks I work too hard and play too little. She's a big-time matchmaker."

"Just like Faith." A pause, and that darn jealousy wave crested inside her again. Kelli wasn't a love interest, but she was a matchmaker. She cringed, but she had to ask. "Did, ah, she make any successful matches for you over the years?"

He cocked his head and studied her. "Wow, you really are jealous. I'm flattered. Would it bother you if she had?"

Cagney pondered that and decided to be honest. "Let's go with…yes." She grimaced. "Sorry. I know I don't have any hold over you."

Jonas leaned his head back and laughed. When he was done guffawing, he grabbed her hand. "That, sweet one, is where you're dead wrong. Let's get some air out on the balcony. It's warm in here."

They snaked their way through the dancing crowd to the balcony on the opposite side of the party room. Cagney wondered if he was ever going to tell her about the Kelli matchmaking thing. Darn it all, she really wanted to know.

"To answer your question…no. Kelli didn't make any matches for me, because

I've stubbornly refused to let her set me up with anyone, much to her chagrin."

Cagney gulped. "Ever?"

"Ever."

Cool peppermint relief tingled over her skin. "Bet Kelli loved that."

"She thinks I'm a giant, stubborn pain in the ass."

"Smart woman," Cagney quipped.

They stepped out into a star-blanketed night on the balcony, settling by the railing. "Actually, she eventually gave up on the whole matchmaking thing and switched gears."

"Meaning?"

"She started nagging me incessantly to reconnect with 'the one who got away,' since I was obviously still hung up on her," he said easily.

Cagney blinked up at him. Moonlight bathed half of his face in a silvery blue while the other half shone gold with the lights spilling out from inside the ballroom. She didn't want to read into his words, but she needed everything to be absolutely above-board between them from here on out. She didn't want to wonder. After moistening her lips with a nervous flick of her tongue, she asked, "The one who ?"

"*You*, Cag," he said, with exaggerated patience. "She nagged me about you. Happy now?"

Warmth radiated through her. She couldn't believe this was happening, but man, was she glad. She practically bounced on her heels. "I'm the one who got away? Kelli thought you were still hung up on me?"

He leaned forward and rested his forehead against hers, still holding her close. "Not thought. Knew. I *am* still hung up on you."

Her heart jolted, then blossomed with a kind of pure joy she hadn't felt in years. "Y-you are?"

"Come on. You have to know it by now." He pulled back and lowered his chin. "I haven't exactly held back in the past few days."

"Yeah, but—" She shook her head. "I thought you hated me when you came back. And the rest of this… wasn't it all for show?"

"No one's that good of an actor, Cag. When I first came back to the Gulch, well, frankly I was an idiot. An angry idiot with a misguided agenda. A hangover from my teen years, maybe. But I have never hated you, even when I tried." He ran the back of his fingers slowly down the side of her face. "Full disclosure, right? We said we owed each other that much."

"Yes," she whispered, her heart pounding.

"This 'for show' stuff served two purposes for me. Piss Chief off—sure. But it also presented a golden opportunity to get closer to you, minus all the risk I feared." He let that admission hang in the air. When he spoke again, his tone had lowered into something velvety and soothing. "I've never gotten over you, Cagney Bishop, even when I tried to tell myself I had. And I never managed to fool Kelli about that."

"Of course not," Cagney said simply, struggling to rein in her soaring emotions. "She's a woman. We're intuitive that way. I should say, *most* of us are," she added wryly. "I, sadly, am lacking in that department. But Kelli's obviously a great friend who can see straight through your…"

"Protective walls?"

"*Bull* was what I was thinking. But protective walls works, too."

He snorted. "I've always hated that female intuition stuff. It's like you women are magical."

"We are, silly."

He raised his eyes heavenward. "Anyway, yes. I admit it, here and now. Every decision I ever made, good, bad or just plain idiotic, was based on the fact that—" He stopped then, and she watched his Adam's apple rise and fall on a nervous swallow.

"What?" she urged. "Just say it."

"That I love you," he said finally, his tone husky.

Her gaze softened. "Jonas." She reached up and wrapped her arms around his neck, kissing him deeply. When they pulled apart, both of them were breathless. "I've always loved you, too. I've never been happier than the day you came back. And it killed me, all this stupid pretending. So, there it is. Full disclosure."

"Full disclosure. No more pretending. Deal?"

She smiled. "The real deal feels good, doesn't it?"

He leaned in and nuzzled her neck, nipping at her ear lobe. "Not nearly as good as it's going to feel later," he said, his words buzzing against her skin.

At her sharp intake of breath, he nipped again.

"You know all those years we lost, Cag?" he drawled against her ear.

"Yes," she managed, though she couldn't seem to breathe.

"We're going to make up for them tonight."

"All in one night? Intriguing."

"I've wanted you since the moment I saw you again, and I don't think I can wait a moment longer."

A small moan escaped before she could press her lips together and cut it off.

"Unless you're opposed to the idea."

"Opposed?" She molded her body against his subtly, but with ultraclear meaning. Her heart thrummed wildly in her chest, but she pulled back and looked directly into his eyes. "I'd take you out of here right this minute to get that particular plan underway if I didn't have to talk to Chief first."

"You have to?"

"Definitely. It's important."

Speak of the devil.

Seemingly appearing out of nowhere, the dark shadow of Chief Bill Bishop suddenly loomed over them, a deep scowl on his face. "What the hell do you think you're doing?" he rasped. "You're making a spectacle of yourself in front of the whole department."

"We're outside," Cagney said, glancing around at the nearly empty space. "On the balcony. Alone."

"Anyone could walk out here. Have a little self-respect. You want them to think of you as some kind of a slut?"

"Watch your mouth, Bill," Jonas said, deadly serious, pulling from his embrace with Cagney to square off with his nemesis.

Chief puffed out his chest in a way that bespoke of authority and also conveyed that omnipresent threat. "Don't tell me how to speak to my daughter."

Jonas didn't back down one millimeter. "Your daughter is an adult who happens to be my date, and she's a classy woman who deserves respect. No one will call her a slut or any other derogatory name in my presence. Not even her father." He scoffed. "I shouldn't have to say that, *especially* her father, but clearly you're an unusual case."

Standoff.

Cagney ignored the exchange. She didn't care what Chief thought. In fact, she didn't care what anyone thought. She was more than ready for this conversation that should've happened years ago. Jonas loved her. She loved Jonas.

Most importantly, she loved herself enough to go through with it. Finally.

She stepped in front of Jonas and pulled

his arms around her middle, facing her father directly. A sense of calm purpose emboldened her. "Where's Mom?"

Chief's scowl deepened. "She didn't come this year."

"Why not?"

"She…wasn't feeling well."

"I'm sorry to hear that. I'll call her later to check on her."

"She's *fine*. You don't need—"

"What, now I can't even call my mother? Is there some reason I shouldn't—or can't—speak to her?"

"I don't appreciate your implication." Chief actually looked flustered. "I didn't do a damn thing to my wife. What kind of monster do you think I am?"

She shook her head sadly. "Trust me, you don't want the answer to that question."

A muscle in his jaw jumped, and he straightened his back. "If you must know, your mother refused to come."

"Good for her. I'm sure she always hated these things." She twisted her head slightly and looked up at Jonas with a smile, then back at her father. "You remember Jonas Eberhardt, don't you, Chief?"

Chief scraped an indignant stare up and

down the two of them. "What kind of inane question is that?"

"Just wanted to make sure." She paused pointedly. "Because I'm in love with him. Always have been, incidentally, but now he's back for good and I'm not going to hide it anymore. If you want any part of my life whatsoever, you're going to start respecting that."

Her father's face purpled with rage, and he shook slightly. "How dare you come to my Ball—"

"Oh, so this event belongs to you now, and not the community?" Cagney asked, with mild curiosity, eyebrows raised. "Just like Mom's your property, and Dee, Terri and me, too? Somehow, your reaction isn't surprising in the least. What is it you object to most, Chief? The fact that Jonas and I are back together, despite your immoral and underhanded attempts to keep us apart? Or the fact that we're together in your face, on your so-called turf?"

Her father's expression remained stony, but the tremor in his hands belied his true feelings. "He never deserved you."

"*You* never deserved me," Cagney countered, in a rough tone. "Or Mom, Terri or

Deirdre. You didn't deserve any of us, and it's making you crazy because you damn well know it. A taste of your own medicine isn't so pleasant, is it?"

"Cut this insolent behavior," he growled lowly. "I mean it. Immediately."

"I don't give a damn what you think of my behavior. Try looking at yourself for once." She pulled out of Jonas's embrace and stepped closer to Chief. "Can you even comprehend what your hatred and bitterness is costing you? You're losing your entire family, one by one."

"Stop this!"

"No, damn it! I won't! Your manipulations and demands can't affect me anymore." She scissored her hands in one clean motion. "I'm done. You've controlled my life for far too long."

"I wanted what was best for you," he growled.

Cagney hiked her chin. "Yeah? Well, I wanted a father who loved me. A real family, one I didn't have to feel ashamed of for my entire life. I wanted sisters I could be close to and a mother I could look up to. But you ruined that. And the saddest part is, you can't even see it."

Chief dropped his gaze briefly, but long enough to fuel Cagney for the rest of the confrontation.

"How about this—we'll leave you to your special night and go home to our own." She cast a meaningful glance at Jonas that was sure to turn her father's stomach. Bonus. "But first, I have something to give you," she said to Chief. She snapped open her evening bag. "Years ago," she said dispassionately, "you passed on a letter supposedly written by me that changed the course of my life. For the worst. I don't suppose that rings a bell?"

Her father's eyes widened in surprise. "Cagney—"

"No. Stop interrupting me, damn it. It's my turn," she said, not caring one iota what her father had to say. She held out a piece of paper that she'd torn from the same purple-lined notebook. It had taken some digging, but she'd found it. She'd never been able to part with any of the things from "the Jonas years." She felt utterly at peace and looked directly into her father's eyes. "The letter you passed on was forged, but I guess I don't have to tell you that. Forgery is a crime, incidentally. Maybe you've been off the streets too long to recall that."

Was it her imagination, or did his face redden?

"Anyway, this one's the real deal. Bona fide." She thrust the letter closer. "Take it, *Daddy*," she said, the word unfamiliar on her tongue since she hadn't uttered it in about twenty-five years. His expression—a mixture of pain and shock—showed that he'd grasped the impact, too. Maybe now he'd start to understand what he'd destroyed with his poisonous thinking, but Cagney wasn't holding her breath. "Trust that this one actually was written by me. For you."

Reluctantly, Chief took the piece of paper, unfolding it slowly. He read it, and the blood drained from his complexion. His gaze shot toward her. "Cagney, don't be ridicu—"

She stopped him with her index finger held up to his face. "Don't you ever—*ever*—try to dictate my life again, Chief. Or you'll lose me completely, like you've lost Terri. Like you've lost so much in your life. You'll be dead to me like your poor, imperfect mother is dead to you, which—not that you asked me—is a damn shame."

Chief's body went rigid and a bead of sweat glistened on his brow. Whether from her harsh words or from the impact of realizing she knew his deepest, darkest secret, she didn't know. And frankly, she didn't care.

She shook her head. "For God's sake, when is it going to end? The dysfunction? The lies? The destruction of our family, all based on bitterness and the past?"

He said nothing.

"Know this. Our family life didn't have to be this way. You created the nightmare, and it was all based on worst-case scenarios conjured up in your mind. *You* did this, from start to finish. Not Mom, not Terri, not me." She didn't feel the need to mention Deirdre. "But you've never taken one shred of responsibility for the destruction. Until you do, nothing will change. Nothing. Our so-called family will remain a pathetic farce, and that's just plain sad, if not downright criminal. I don't think I can ever forgive you for it."

Chief's lips thinned into a grim line, but again, he remained stonily silent.

Cagney accepted that for the victory it was. She turned, head held high, back straight, and took Jonas's hand. "Come on, love. I've had my fill of the Ball, and I've done what I came here to do. Take me home."

They strode through the ballroom hand-in-hand, but didn't speak until Jonas had passed over the valet ticket and the two of them stood on the curb alone waiting for the car to arrive.

"Wow," Jonas said, with wonder and admiration in his tone. "I mean…wow."

She exhaled all the pain of her life in one long breath. "You can say that again."

"You okay?"

"Are you kidding? I'm fantastic."

"Well, I'm completely impressed. Stunned, but impressed."

Cagney sniffed. "It needed to be done. Long ago, actually, but better late than never."

He wrapped one arm around her shoulder. "Can I ask what the letter said?"

"Just one short sentence." She hiked a shoulder. "Something I should've said years ago. Unfortunately I didn't have the drive to do so until you came back."

"Tell me what it said," Jonas said softly.

"The two most freeing words of my life." She looked at him directly, her lips spreading into a triumphant smile. "It said, 'I quit.'"

Chapter Twelve

"Stop asking me if I'm sure," Cagney told Jonas as she unlocked the front door to the teen center. "I've never felt so fantastic in my life, okay? Handing Chief that letter was one of the most gratifying and empowering things I've ever done, so stop worrying."

He couldn't help it. The fact that she'd resigned right there at the Police Ball left him dumbstruck. Proud, but taken aback, and more than a little guilt-ridden, truth be told. "I don't want to be the cause of you throwing away a ten-year career, that's all."

She turned to face him, pulling him inside

and locking the door behind them. She pushed him against the door and held him there. His muscles tensed in an exhilarating way. Damn if he didn't like this aggressive side to her. All new, but very welcome and arousing.

"Jonas, listen to me. I'm only going to say this once."

"All ears."

"I *never* wanted to be a cop. Ever." She flicked her hand dismissively. "Sure, okay, I was good at it. Whatever. But I wasn't happy, and isn't that the point of life? Being happy?"

"I'm starting to believe that's true."

She pressed her body against his and reached up to nibble his bottom lip. "One day, I'll lay out the whole ugly story of how I got roped into police work for you so you'll understand why resigning was so easy for me." She paused, meeting his gaze directly. "But right now I want you naked. In my bed. I've waited way too long for this, and I don't want to talk, I want to make love. Okay?"

Jonas's body throbbed. He slid one hand down her back and pressed her pelvis into him more firmly, making it ultraclear that he wanted the same thing. "Gotta say, Cag, tell years on the job have given you a directness that drives me absolutely crazy. In a good way."

She smiled slowly. "Yeah?"

He leaned down to capture her mouth with his. For several minutes, they explored each other while braced against the door... kissing, touching, murmuring their desires and needs to each other in rushed, urgent tones and raw, sexy language. But they were still on the ground level—the teen center— and they both knew it.

Not quite the ambience either of them wanted.

Cagney broke away, grabbing his hand. "Come on."

In the freight elevator, they continued their exploration against the back wall. When the car lurched to a stop at the second floor, she lowered her chin. "You are *not* continuing up to the guest suite. Just FYI."

"How could a man argue with that?"

They disembarked together, scarcely able to keep their hands off of each other. Her stilettos were the first to go, kicked aside in the living-room area. He tossed his jacket and cummerbund over the kitchen island, his shirt at the bedroom door. By then she had her hair pins pulled out, and he was busy kicking off his shoes and unzipping his pants.

"You're going to have to take this dress off me."

"Music to my ears." He spun her against the wall, running with her aggressive lead, and the sound of that zipper that ran from her neckline to her shapely bottom reverberated through his mind like the most exquisite aphrodisiac. He slid his hands into the dress and around to cup her breasts, startled to find them naked and peaked with desire.

He swallowed. "You're not wearing a bra."

"A woman doesn't wear a bra with a dress like this, Jonas," she said, reaching up to press his hands more firmly against her. "It ruins the line. I'm not wearing much down below, either—same reason."

"Much?" he asked, in a lust-choked tone.

"Find out for yourself," she challenged.

His urgency amped up to the uncontrollable level. He could hardly see. Smoothing his palms over her flat, soft tummy, he made his way to the smallest pair of thong underwear he'd ever imagined. They covered the front, but the back consisted of miniscule T-shaped strings. "Cagney."

"Take them off. Take it all off." She spun

to face him. "Now. I want you inside me more than I've ever wanted anything in my life, and forgive me for being forward, but I think I've waited long enough. We both have."

His hands shook now, with anticipation and arousal from her straightforward demands. "I don't suppose you'll talk dirty to me, too?"

"I'll do anything you want once we're naked."

He did as she asked, pushing her dress to the floor in a heap, then hooking her T-back underwear with his thumbs and pulling them to her ankles, as well. He stopped before her to kiss what the underwear had uncovered, ecstatic to find her wet and swollen with desire.

She ran her hand through his hair, and he looked up at her. "Foreplay can come later, Jonas." He must've looked confused, because she added, "I know, I know—a woman's not supposed to say that. But just this time, I want you to take me, hard and fast. No holding back. Okay?"

He stood, quickly shedding the rest of his clothing. His body throbbed for her so intensely, it was actually painful. Painful ecstasy.

Within moments, he'd eased her backward onto the bed, covering her with his own body. He hesitated, gazing into the depths of her eyes.

Beneath him, she spread her legs, and he could feel the wet heat pressing against him. "Now."

"Cagney—"

"Jonas, *now*. All of you. I need you inside me. Don't make me resort to the rougher language I want to use." She quirked an eyebrow. "I'm trying to maintain some semblance of being a lady here."

He chuckled. "I think we're past that."

"What are you waiting for, then?" She opened her legs wider and ground against him, reaching between them to wrap her hand around his rock hardness, guiding him where she wanted him.

"God, Cag."

She released him.

He rose up, then thrust deeply into her body, thrilled to feel her body clench and spasm around him.

Groaning, Cagney arched her back and intensified the connection, rotating her hips in a way that brought stars to his vision.

He met her thrust for thrust, obeying her

every demand for harder, faster, deeper. Her fingernails were short, but she managed to dig them into his back muscles despite that, and it only increased his pleasure.

Their joining was just what she'd demanded.

Hot.

Fast.

Hard.

Complete.

They climaxed together, each crying out and pulled taut like piano strings about to snap. He stayed tensed until the pulsating inside her eased to a lulling sense of contentment, and then he relaxed on top of her, both of them breathing heavily.

"Incredible," she whispered.

"Better than ever. More than any fantasy, Cag, I swear."

She hugged him as tightly as possible with her weakened arms. "The best is yet to come, honey. I'm nowhere near finished with you yet."

He moaned. "God, you may kill me before the night's over."

"If that, uh, *performance,* was any indication, I think you can take the heat, and then some."

He grinned. "Glad you think so."

She laughed beneath him, the deep, lulling sound of a woman well loved. "Hey, look at the bright side. If we do kill each other in the process, what a way to go."

Jonas eased into wakefulness the next morning, his head on a pillow that smelled like Cagney—crisp pine, gently swaying wildflowers, and one hundred percent woman.

And then, key areas of his body reminded him of the mind-blowing sensual connection they shared last night. He smiled before he even opened his eyes, thinking it would be a great idea to pull her into his arms, all warm and drowsy, and wake her up properly. Much more satisfying than an alarm and a finer jolt than the best Italian espresso.

Cagney Bishop and Jonas Eberhardt.

After all these years, so much pain.

Who would've believed it?

Their night together had been…everything he could've hoped for and yet nothing he'd ever imagined. Shared history combined with the fact that they'd both grown up and into their own sexuality had proven explosive and poignant, almost too much to wrap his brain around. All he knew at this point was he wanted more.

His body stirred, reliving their explosive lovemaking in his mind, and he reached out for her.

She wasn't there.

He lifted his head to check; sure enough, Cagney's side of the bed was empty, but he smelled coffee and heard soft music wafting in from the other room. She always had been an early riser.

Jonas threw the covers back and pulled on his boxer briefs and tuxedo pants—an odd choice for morning loungewear, he knew, but it was all he had on this level of the loft. He took a moment to study the matted and framed poems he'd written for her back in high school that graced the wall above the headboard. He'd been stunned, so touched, when he'd noticed them during one of their breathers the night before. More than any words she could ever say, those framed pieces of notebook paper proved she still loved him, that she'd always loved him, despite everything.

They made him want to write again.

Dream again.

Live again.

She made him want all that and more. He ran his fingers gently along one of the frames, full to bursting with emotions that needed outlet on the page.

He padded barefoot and bare-chested to the bedroom door and eased it open. Morning light flooded the loft, making everything in it gleam. It seemed vast and homey at the same time. Only a true artist could have pulled off that combination. He glanced around the wide-open space until he spotted Cagney, seated by the north-facing windows, quietly absorbed in painting.

His heart clenched.

He leaned against the doorjamb and studied her. Her facial expression as serene as an angel's, she wore his tuxedo shirt—barely buttoned, with the sleeves rolled up above her elbows—and nothing more. Her long hair, still mussed from sleep and love-making, cascaded down her back in a golden fall.

God, her beauty dazzled him.

She looked all the more beautiful doing what she'd been born to do: create art. If the bliss that surrounded her like an aura was any indication, quitting the job she claimed she'd never really loved had been the best choice she'd ever made—second to forgiving him for every stupid thing he'd ever done, that is. He dismissed his worry about her sudden resignation the night before.

He adjusted his stance, and the floor-board creaked.

Cagney glanced up. "Hey," she said, a private lover's smile tilting the corners of her lips.

"Hey, yourself." He pushed off the door-jamb and started toward her.

"What were you doing?" she asked.

"Watching you. Stunned by your beauty."

"Flattery will get you everywhere," she teased.

"It's not flattery. It's fact. What are you doing?"

"What I should've been doing long ago. Painting."

"Can I see?"

She shook her head. "Sorry. Surely you remember how I am about my works in progress." Setting her brush and palette down carefully, she crossed the room and met him in the middle, leaning into him and tilting her face up for a deep, passionate morning kiss.

"Mmm," he said. "Good morning to you, too. You're wearing my shirt."

She clutched the lapels, raising them to her face. "It smells like you. Do you mind?"

"Are you crazy?"

She laughed. "Do you know how long I've dreamt of this?" she said, sliding her arms around his waist.

He nestled her head beneath his chin and took a deep breath, easing it out. "Yeah, I think I do know."

"So, what now?"

He planted a kiss on her forehead. "Well, much as I'd like to barricade myself in the loft with you forever—"

"And make love until we're medically unable to continue?"

He chuckled. "Yes. That. However, work must go on."

She clicked her tongue. "It's Saturday. Saturday's a go-back-to-bed day."

"I know. But I have a few things to take care of at the hospital that can't wait."

She pouted briefly, then let it go. "Okay. Will you come back soon?"

He ran his hands down the curvy shape of her body, making clear his intentions for later. "Nothing could keep me away, Casey Laine Bishop. Not anymore."

Cagney was so engrossed in painting that the buzz of the doorbell startled her. She jolted, smearing a large swath of cerulean blue across the canvas, swore, then set her tools aside. She could fix the error later. That was the beauty of painting.

Before crossing to the intercom, she glanced out the window. All she saw was a taxi van idling at the curb.

She frowned. Strange. Thank goodness she'd thrown on a pair of jeans after Jonas had left.

She hurried to the intercom and pressed the button. "Yes?"

"Cagney, honey, it's me," came her mom's voice. "Are you busy? Or can I come up for a few minutes."

Cagney smiled. "Of course you can come up." But confusion swirled through her brain. What was her mom doing in a taxi van? She pushed the button to buzz her mom in, then anxiously awaited the arrival of the freight elevator.

The enormous car ground to a halt at the second level, and Cagney pulled open the door. "This is a surprise."

Helen, glowing like she never had before, smiled over the large box she struggled beneath. "I had to speak to you before I left."

"Left?" More befuddlement. Cagney

stepped forward. "Here, let me take that box from you. What on earth—?"

"In due time." Helen brushed off her clothes. "Boy, that was heavier than I'd anticipated."

Cagney set it aside and embraced her mom. "It's good to see you. Would you like some coffee? Water?"

"No, sweetie, that's fine. I don't have much time."

An odd sort of fluttering took hold of her tummy. "Mom, what's going on?"

Helen settled onto the couch with a sigh. "I hear you resigned from the PD."

Cagney swallowed through a suddenly tight throat. "Yes. Was Chief flaming pissed?"

Helen laughed. "You could put it that way." She patted the cushion next to her. "Sit with me."

Cagney did.

Helen took her daughter's hands in her own. "I'm proud of you. You're finally following your passion. Your dreams. And that's what you should do. You're no longer fearful of your father, which is such a positive step."

"Mom," Cagney said, her voice wobbling, "you're scaring me. What's this all about?"

Helen squeezed, then released Cagney's hands. "Your father and I had it out again last night after the Ball."

"You didn't go."

Helen shrugged. "I don't want to play the game anymore." She reached over and touched Cagney's nose. "You taught me that, honey."

"But, what does that mean?"

Helen took in a deep breath. "Your father and I are separating."

Unexpectedly, Cagney's stomach dropped. She should feel thrilled. Why didn't she? "But—what are you going to do?"

Helen laughed, free and calm. "That's the beauty of it. Who knows? I'll let it play out as I go."

Cagney hated herself for asking this, but she couldn't see any way around it. Oddly, she wanted to know. "Is Chief okay?"

"I wouldn't say okay. But he made his bed," Helen said. "I'm not at the point of divorce, mind you, but I'm taking time away to explore who exactly Helen Bishop is. Seems I've lost little bits of myself over the years. I need to find them, then figure out if your father and I have anything left."

"Mom…I'm sorry."

"Don't be, Cagney. I should've done this long ago."

"Where will you go?" Cagney asked, stunned to realize she wanted to cry.

Helen cast a glance at the box she'd brought. "That's the thing. The reason I came. Well, other than to say goodbye for now."

That was it. Cagney's tears demanded release. She and her mom hadn't been close for years, if ever, but just when they'd begun to repair their tattered relationship, Mom was leaving.

Her mom cupped her face. "Honey, don't cry. I'm following your lead, summoning my inner strength."

"But I don't want you to go."

"It's not forever, sweet girl. I promise."

"Where are you going?" Cagney reiterated.

"Terri has invited me to come stay with her in New York City. I've always wanted to go there."

How much shock could one person take? Cagney's hands started to shake. "Y-you talked to Terri?"

Helen lowered her chin. "I never stopped talking to Terri. That's my deep, dark secret."

A stunned silence ensued. Cagney didn't

know whether to be angry or thrilled. "W-what do you mean?"

"I know I came off as submissive and ineffectual all these years, but I had my private time, and I made good use of it." Helen tilted her head toward the box. "That box is filled with letters from Terri, in chronological order. I want you to have them. Read them. Get to know your sister again."

"But how—?"

"Private post office box." Her mom shrugged. "I gave in to him on most issues, but I wasn't going to lose one of my daughters, no matter what he said."

Cagney clasped her hands together at chest level. "Oh, Mom. I can't believe—"

"I've also included all the contact information for Grandma Leila," she said with a sniff. "You don't have to, but I hope you'll keep in contact with the care packages until I come back."

"Of course. You know I will."

Helen smiled, then her expression turned wistful. "I have to go. I don't want to miss my flight, you know."

Suddenly desperate, Cagney reached out and grasped her mom's forearm. "Wait. What's Terri been doing?"

"It's all in the box, honey." Helen stood. "You have all our contact information, too. And you're always welcome to visit, although I think you should spend some quality time with that man of yours."

Cagney choked up, then stood and pulled her mom into a fierce hug. "I love you. Please tell Terri I love her, too. And miss her. So much."

Helen kissed her cheek. "I will. Come to New York. You and Jonas."

"We will."

The taxi driver honked, and the two pulled apart.

"I always thought you were weak, Mom." Cagney's cheeks heated. "I'm sorry for that. I was wrong."

"Oh, I don't know. I may have been weaker than I could've been," Helen said. "But those days are over." She placed her hands on either side of Cagney's face. "And you have nothing, ever, to apologize for."

After another quick embrace, her mother was gone.

Cagney stared at the box for mere seconds before she retrieved a knife from the kitchen to slice open the tape. She gasped when she opened it; a veritable mother lode of correspondence. Her painting forgotten, she sat cross-legged on the floor and dug in.

Amazing.

After being stuck in a rut for more than a decade, she'd taken a few brave steps, and just like that, life was changing all around her. Her mother had struck out on her own, she had a lifeline to Terri.

Most of all, Jonas was back in her life.

For a moment, Cagney simply basked in the wonder and bliss of it all. And then, with a smile on her face and tears in her eyes, she pulled out the oldest of the letters and started reading.

Jonas breezed through his work at the hospital in record time, anxious to return to Cagney's side. Once inside his car, though, he felt the urgent need for guidance. They'd taken some huge steps, but what next?

He pulled his cell phone from his belt and dialed the familiar number. It rang three times.

"Paradise Central," Tony said when he answered. Zydeco music thumped in the background, and clearly his best friends were having the time of their lives.

Jonas grinned. "You've got this good-life thing down, man. Gotta tell you."

"Jonas!" Tony exclaimed, true joy in his tone. "I wondered when you'd call. What the hell's going on, bro?"

"Same old. You know." He paused, then cleared his throat. "Can I, ah, talk to Kelli?"

Tony snorted. "Same old, my ass. Hang on."

After some shuffling, Kelli came on the line. "Jonas, honey! Did you change your mind about flying out to Antigua?"

"Not exactly," he hedged.

She sucked in a breath. "Oh, my God. You did it! You kicked your ego to the curb and reconciled with her, didn't you? Tell me right now before I burst."

"Things are going...well." He heard her clapping in the background.

"That's beautiful, J. Gorgeous. I'm so proud of you. Now, tell all. I've waited for this forever."

How could he encapsulate everything that had happened in one short conversation? He settled for the core truth, hoping it would suffice. "I love her, Kelli."

"Duh," Kelli said with a laugh. "What are you going to do about it?"

He pressed his lips together. "That's what I'm calling you for. Advice."

"Men." Kelli sighed dramatically. "Helpless, I swear. Does she love you, too?"

"Yes." The corners of his mouth raised into a smug and proud smile. "She matted and framed love poems I wrote for her in high school. High school, Kel. They actually hang above her bed."

"Awww! That's so perfect on a couple of levels. One, *so* romantic—oh, my God, I can't even say. And two, you've obviously been in her bed."

Jonas squirmed. "We, um…"

"I'm not going to push you for details. Just answer one thing, honey. Pure honesty. Is this a forever kind of situation?" Kelli asked, her voice soft.

He didn't even have to think about it. "Absolutely."

"Then, geez! What do you need with me? You know exactly what to do next." She paused meaningfully. "Don't you?"

Silence stretched between them, but for the zydeco music in the background.

Damned if he didn't know. Kelli was a genius. His heart filled and lifted. "I love you, Kel. You're the best."

She laughed with her signature effervescence. "Don't you forget it. I want to meet her, Jonas. Soon."

"You will."

"Good. Now go make that woman yours forever, and do it in a big way."

"Okay."

"She's always been yours anyway," Kelli said, with that cool insight again. "You just needed to get out of your own stubborn way."

Problem.

He wanted to do it right.

And no offense to Damiani Jewelers, but he had his mind's eye on something spectacular, something he'd have to fly to Paris or London or Los Angeles—maybe even Antigua—to find. Damiani did have what he needed for the time being, however, and he took care of it in short order.

The moment he slipped his key into the lock of the teen center, his heart began to thud. Was it always this way? The fear? Apprehension? Excitement?

He pulled open the massive doors to the freight elevator, entered, then pushed the button for level two. As the car ascended, his throat dried up. Maybe this was lame.

Maybe he was a complete idiot. He eyed the emergency stop button, but didn't go for it.

Buck up, Eberhardt.

He knew Cagney; he had to remember that.

When the elevator stopped on Cagney's floor, a sense of calm, of rightness settled over him. He pulled open the door, and the love of his life glanced up. She sat on the floor in the middle of a huge scatter of letters. "My sister is a big-time literary agent in New York City," she said without preamble.

He blinked. "Excuse me?"

Her words came in a rush, eyes bright, cheeks flushed. "Terri. She and my mom have kept in touch all this time, behind Chief's back, and now Mom's going to live with her in New York City because she and Chief have separated. But she brought me this box of letters—Mom, I mean—and it's like a chronicle of all I've missed—"

He hadn't been aware of his grin.

"What?"

"I love seeing you so happy, so excited."

Cagney set down the letter she'd been reading and regrouped. "Wait. I'm sorry. I was being self-centered. How did everything go at the hospital?"

"Everything's perfect." He crossed the room and sat on the floor with her. "Go on. Tell me about Terri."

A playful wariness overtook her expression. "Later. What's on your mind?"

"How do you know I have something on my mind?"

"Duh?"

He shook his head. "Man, first Kelli, now you. This women's intuition stuff is freaky."

Her eyes widened. "You spoke with Kelli?"

"And Tony. They want to meet you. How do you feel about a trip to Antigua?"

She scoffed. "I feel desperate for a trip to Antigua, but you'll recall, I'm unemployed."

"Ah, yes. About that." He reached behind him and extracted some papers from the back pocket of his jeans. "I took the liberty of researching some distance education programs for counseling while I was at the hospital." He handed them over.

She leafed through them, then peered up at him quizzically. "What's this about?"

"I want you to work at the teen center and, eventually, with the art therapy program full-time. You were meant to do it, Cag." He shrugged. "This is one way to get your certification without having to leave the Gulch."

She swallowed. "Are you offering me a job?"

"If you're interested."

Laughter burst from her. "Are you kidding? Of course I'm interested. Am I allowed to sleep with the boss?"

"I wouldn't have it any other way."

She lifted he papers. "This was really thoughtful of you, Jonas."

"Wait. I'd like to offer you something else, too."

Confusion changed her expression.

He handed over the small, white cardboard box. "It's just the first in a long line, and it's not much, but—"

"Shhh. Stop explaining. Just let me just open it."

With slightly shaky hands, she removed the box top to find a sterling silver charm for her bracelet—a pair of interlocked wedding bands. After staring into the box for several excruciating moments, she raised her gaze to meet his. "Jonas, what does this mean?"

"It means I want to buy you an engagement ring, but it has to be the perfect ring. Because you're the perfect woman for me."

"E-engagement?" she asked, her voice thin.

He moved closer, gently setting the charm

box aside and taking her hands in his own. "I know it's not an award-winning proposal, Cag, but it's all I have right now, and I can't wait anymore. I want to do this right, honey. We can fly somewhere and pick out a ring. Anywhere you want. Paris, London, Antwerp, Los Angeles—"

"New York City," she said.

"The Big Apple it is. But I'm asking now." He paused to swallow and moisten his lips. "Casey Laine Bishop, please do me the honor of being my wife. Let's live together, work together. Explore the world together. Say yes. Please."

Her face absolutely glowed. She removed one hand and retrieved the charm box. "Put it on."

She held out her wrist.

He looked from the charm bracelet to her eyes. "You haven't taken it off? It's a trinket, Cag."

"Maybe so, but it's the most precious trinket I've ever received, and I'll *never* take it off."

In silence, he attached the new charm to the bracelet, then raised her hand to his mouth for a gentle kiss.

She raised her wrist, twisting it about to

admire the charm. "You're amazing, Jonas. You always know just what to do. You may not think this is the perfect proposal, but I do. It couldn't be more perfect."

His heart resumed the steady thud. "Does that mean—?"

She threw herself into his arms. "Yes, yes, yes! I can think of nothing better than being your wife, working alongside you, building a life."

He pulled back and studied her face. "I have never loved another woman, Cagney. You've been my beginning and my middle, and, God willing, you'll be my end."

"I love you, too. So incredibly much."

They kissed then, tenderly.

"A new start?"

"Absolutely." She sighed. "I'm so glad you're back in my world."

He ran his fingers down her soft cheek. "You, love, aren't *in* my world, you *are* my world."

She eased him back onto the letter-piled floor, then covered his body with her own. "It doesn't get better than that, does it?"

"I say we give it a try."

She lowered her lips to his, and every single wound from the past healed for both

of them as they melted into the future.
Together.

The way it always should've been.

Epilogue

Opening day at the teen center was pure, blissful pandemonium. The whole town turned out, it seemed, but more importantly, Terri, Deirdre and Mom had all flown in to commemorate the ribbon cutting.

Noticeably absent? Chief Bill Bishop.

Tony and Kelli had come, too, after Cagney and Jonas had flown to Antigua for a long weekend. Cagney had adored Kelli on sight. The woman's enthusiasm was contagious, and now that she'd come to the Gulch, all Cagney's friends had welcomed her into the fold.

Best of all, the previously skeptical teens were digging the place fully—so gratifying after their near miss.

Cagney worked the room, accepted effusive hugs and congratulations from hundreds of people.

But something was missing for her.

She felt an emptiness, a wrong turn.

It took her half the morning to figure it out, but once the answer popped startlingly into her head, she knew exactly what she needed to do. Excusing herself, she headed upstairs for a moment and retrieved a monogramed note card from her writing desk.

Taking a deep breath, she sat down and grabbed her favorite pen. She dithered over what to say for a few moments, and then realized simple was best.

With a steady hand, she wrote:

Dad,
I forgive you.
Your daughter, Casey Laine

With a sense of peace coursing through her, she sealed the envelope, addressed it, then slipped back downstairs and outside. By some fluke, Beverly, their mail carrier, was just depositing the day's deliveries into her mailbox. The older woman glanced up and smiled when she saw Cagney.

"Well, hello, doll." She lifted her chin toward the teen center. "Looks like a rousing success."

"It is. You should come in and have some cake."

"No can do. I've got my route, gotta stick to schedule."

"I understand," Cagney said. "You'll stop by another time?"

"Of course."

Cagney took in a deep breath and eased it out. "I have this for you." She held out the note card.

"Perfect timing, huh?" Beverly said, tucking the card into her messenger bag without even looking at it. "I love when that happens. It's like mail karma."

"Mail karma happens when it's supposed to," Cagney said, fully grasping the layers of meaning in that statement. She aimed one thumb over her shoulder. "I have to get back."

"You should be proud of yourself, doll. What you've accomplished here—" Beverly shook her head in wonder. "The pride of Troublesome Gulch."

"Thank you, Beverly. Truly."

Back inside, her disconcerted feelings from earlier completely gone, Cagney quickly found Jonas and wound her arms around his body from behind.

He grasped her forearms and pulled her closer. "Hey," he said, a smile in his tone as he glanced over his shoulder. "Where have you been? I've been looking for you."

"Letting go of the past," she said. "For good this time, so I can start my future with you."

He turned until they were face-to-face, embracing. A line of concern bisected his forehead. "What do you mean? You okay?"

"Absolutely. Better than ever. I just had something I needed to do." *Namely, breaking a cycle that had gone on way too long.* It was the final step for her.

"But everything's good?"

"Everything's perfect." She tipped her face up for a kiss that held promise. "Now, let's go celebrate our success."

"And our freedom," Jonas said.

"And our love."

"Our forever love," he said.

"Yes. Finally." She kissed him again, then laughed—whole and clear and more at peace than she'd ever been.

* * * * *